Stirs Up More Trouble

Riley Mack

Stirs Up More Trouble

CHRIS GRABENSTEIN

HARPER

An Imprint of HarperCollinsPublishers

Riley Mack Stirs Up More Trouble

Library of Congress Cataloging-in-Publication Data
Grabenstein, Chris.
    Riley Mack stirs up more trouble / Chris Grabenstein.
        p.   cm.
    Summary: "Riley Mack and his friends are back in action—
making trouble in the name of justice—this time to stop a
pollution cover-up and protect one of their own from talent-show
sabotage"— Provided by publisher.
    ISBN 978-0-06-202622-4 (hardback)
    [1. Heroes—Fiction. 2. Schools—Fiction. 3. Friend-
ship—Fiction. 4. Pollution—Fiction. 5. Talent shows—Fiction.
6. Mystery and detective stories.]   I. Title.
PZ7.G7487Ris 2013   2012022148
[Fic]—dc23   CIP
                                                  AC

Typography by Erin Fitzsimmons
13 14 15 16 17   CG/RRDH   10 9 8 7 6 5 4 3 2 1
❖
First Edition

FOR SCHAACK VAN DEUSEN,
THE TEACHER WHO TAUGHT ME
THAT READING AND WRITING COULD BE COOL.

AND, OF COURSE, JJ

Stirs Up More Trouble

PROLOGUE

SAVANNAH MUNHOLLAND SAT STARING AT the extremely strange message her fellow fifth grader Jamal Wilson had handed her right before she stepped into the room to serve her first ever detention:

If anyone asks, you wrote the letter.

She had no idea what it meant.

"Ms. Munholland?" snapped Mr. Ball, the assistant principal. "What are you reading?"

"Nothing, sir."

"Do you have homework?"

"Yes, sir."

"Then do it!"

"But, sir, I have to go home. I can't be here."

1

The assistant principal rubbed his thumb in tiny circles over his index finger. "Do you know what this is, Ms. Munholland?"

"No, sir."

"The smallest record player in the world playing 'My Heart Bleeds for You.'"

"But, my mom's at work, sir. I need to be at the house when my little sister comes home from school. . . ."

"Maybe you should've thought about your family responsibilities before you wore that shirt to school."

Savannah looked down at her olive drab T-shirt. It had WELL-BEHAVED WOMEN RARELY MAKE HISTORY silk-screened across the front.

"My mom gave me this. She loves history. She's a librarian."

"Really? Then tell her to head over to the reference section and look up *school dress code*. Fairview Middle will not tolerate rabble-rousing slogans plastered across T-shirts. No, sir. Not on my watch!"

Savannah slumped down in her seat. Her poor sister. Hailey was only in the third grade and if nobody was home when she got off the bus . . .

Suddenly, the overhead intercom speaker buzzed to life.

"Mr. Ball?"

"Yes, Mrs. James? What is it?"

"Sorry to bother you sir, but, well, Principal Fowler

just received a very interesting telephone call."

"What?"

"It was from that TV show!" The school secretary sounded superthrilled. *"America's Most Talented Teachers."*

Suddenly, the classroom door swung open to reveal Hubert Montgomery (a seventh grader so huge, he looked like he had seven other seventh graders stuffed inside him).

"Wow. Did somebody just mention *America's Most Talented Teachers*? That's my favorite . . . TV show!"

"Mr. Montgomery?"

"Yes, Mr. Ball?"

"Are you serving detention this afternoon?"

"No, sir," the big bear said sheepishly. "I was just out here. At my locker. And I heard Mrs. James mention my all-time favorite . . . TV talent show."

Assistant Principal Ball ripped an orange detention slip off a thick pad on his desk. "Would you like to join us today?"

"No, thank you, sir. Sorry, sir."

Montgomery backed out of the room and shut the door.

"Mr. Ball?" said the voice through the intercom speaker. *"America's Most Talented Teachers* is *the* top-rated show on Disney's Education Channel!"

"Really? Then why haven't I ever heard of it?"

"Well, they've certainly heard of you!"

"What?"

"They want to put you on the show as a contestant. You could win fifty thousand dollars plus new uniforms for the band!"

Mr. Ball tugged at his tie and sort of smiled. "Really?" All of a sudden, he didn't sound so grouchy. "Free band uniforms?"

"Yes, sir. I hope you don't mind, but I gave the producer—a young lady with a British accent named Abigail Rose Painter—your cell phone number."

Just then, a cell phone blared the theme song from *Dancing with the Stars.*

"Oh, I'll bet that's her!" said Mrs. James excitedly.

Mr. Ball unclipped his BlackBerry from its belt holster. He quickly studied the caller ID screen and cleared his throat.

"Hello, Ms. Painter, this is Assistant Principal Albert Ball at Fairview Middle School. How may I be of assistance?"

Savannah and the other kids in detention hall sat in stunned silence while Mr. Ball chatted with the television producer.

"Uhm-hmm. I see. Fifty thousand dollars, eh? *And* band uniforms? Well, I'm honored. If you don't mind my asking, how did you folks hear about me? Really? Is that so?"

Suddenly, Mr. Ball was staring at Savannah.

And, he was smiling!

"Perhaps she heard me sing at last winter's barbershop quartet event out at the mall. Hmm? The finals are in Hollywood? Really?" Now Mr. Ball was actually chuckling. "Well, no, Ms. Painter—I've never flown *anywhere* first-class. Uhm-hmm. Thank you. You, too."

Mr. Ball slid his BlackBerry back into its belt clip and motioned for Savannah to come join him up at his desk.

"Yes, Mr. Ball?" she said in a nervous whisper.

"Did you really write a letter to the folks at *America's Most Talented Teachers*?"

Savannah remembered the strange note Jamal Wilson had handed her.

"Yes, sir. I wrote the letter."

"They might want you to be on the show, too."

"Really?"

"To answer a few questions. About me and my singing, of course." Mr. Ball started humming happily and opened his detention ledger. "Now then, seeing how this is your first offense and weighing the extra credit you should have earned by engaging in this commendable extracurricular activity with the television people, I hereby commute your sentence to time served."

Savannah glanced up at the clock. She'd only been in detention hall for five minutes.

"You are free to go," said Mr. Ball, grandly gesturing toward the door. "I hope, when talking to the folks at *America's Most Talented Teachers*, you will remember how I always strive to find the perfect harmony between justice and mercy."

"Yes, sir."

Savannah hurried out the door and into the hall.

That's when she saw Briana Bloomfield, the star of just about every play or musical at the middle school, tucking the same kind of push-button microphone the principal used in the office to make announcements into her backpack. Meanwhile Jake Lowenstein, another seventh grader and total technogeek, sat on Hubert Montgomery's gigantic shoulders so he could fiddle with some brightly colored wires connected to a black box under a popped-up ceiling panel.

"Assistant Principal Ball?" Briana said with a very thick, very warbly British accent into her cell phone. "Abigail Rose Painter. Sorry to bother you again, sir, but Chip Dale—he's the star of our show—would *love* to chat with you, one-on-one. Perhaps sample a bit of your singing?"

Jamal Wilson came bopping up the hall.

"Okay, Savannah," he whispered. "Briana will keep Mr. Ball tied up for a few more minutes. You need to grab your bike and hurry home." He took her by the elbow and led her toward the front of the school.

"Your little sister Hailey will be the last one dropped off today."

"H-h-how . . ."

"Seems the bus driver owes Riley Mack a favor. Something to do with stopping kids from spitballing her in the back of her head."

"Did Riley . . . ?"

"Yep. He orchestrated this whole operation. I, of course, provided valuable assistance. Even came up with the idea for the TV show. Mr. Ball loves to sing in the faculty bathroom when he thinks no one is listening."

Savannah looked over her shoulder and saw Jake Lowenstein and Hubert Montgomery packing up the last of their gear. Briana was still on her cell.

"Al?" she said into her phone, sounding a lot like Ryan Seacrest. "This is Chip Dale. I'd *love* to hear you sing something, buddy."

Savannah realized that even the voice of Mrs. James, the school secretary on the intercom, had really been Briana Bloomfield!

Inside the classroom, Mr. Ball started bellowing something about "Sweet Adeline, my Adeline" and how at night "For you I pine!" He was singing so loud, Savannah could hear him all the way up the corridor to the front door.

When she and Jamal stepped outside, Riley Mack—

his red hair blazing in the sunshine, his arms folded casually across his chest—was leaning up against the bicycle rack waiting for them.

"You better head home," he said. "Hailey will be there soon."

"Thank you guys so much!" gushed Savannah.

Riley shrugged nonchalantly. "We saw a wrong and tried to right it. It's what we do."

"And, in my humble opinion," added Jamal, "we do it better than anyone in the world. Except maybe those guys from *Mission Impossible*. They're pretty good, too."

RILEY MACK'S EXTRAORDINARILY awesome talents weren't the kind he could showcase on TV or at a school talent show.

If he did, he might end up in detention hall.

For life.

But a talent show was why Riley and his mom were eating Sunday brunch at Fairview's hoity-toity Brookhaven Country Club.

Brunch, Riley had discovered, was a meal halfway between breakfast and lunch. If you ate between lunch and dinner, he figured they called it dunch. Or linner.

"How are your eggs Benedict?" asked Mr. Paxton, the country club president and the guy who had invited

Riley and his mom to the stuffy old mansion where men wore ties and blazers to breakfast.

"Delicious," said Riley's mother.

Riley had ordered chicken fingers and french fries off the Little Putters kids menu, even though he was twelve. He just couldn't stand the sight of eggs Benedict: wobbly poached eggs plopped on top of an English muffin, then smothered in yellow gunk that made it look like the cook had blown a noseful of boogers all over your breakfast.

"Is this your first visit to Brookhaven, Mrs. Mack?" asked Mr. Paxton, who sounded even snottier than the eggs looked.

"Yes," his mother answered. "We've driven past, of course, but we've never actually been inside before. Everything is so beautiful!"

The country club dining room looked like the kind of place a mom would want to be taken on Mother's Day. Real wooden chairs, not scooped-out plastic seats like the ones at Burger King. Tablecloths. Oil paintings of foxhunts on the walls. With his shaggy red hair the color of fox fur, Riley always rooted for the hunted to outfox the hunters, horses, and hounds.

"Well, as I've said, I hope you'll come back in two weeks to help us judge the talent competition," said Mr. Paxton. "It'll be part of our Grand Reopening Gala when we finish renovating all the greens and fairways."

Totally bored, Riley glanced out the big bay window and watched a mustard-yellow backhoe—half trench-digger and half bulldozer—rumble across a rolling lawn he wouldn't want to mow. It would take, like, a week. Maybe a month.

"In thirteen days, the golf course will reopen," Mr. Paxton droned on, "and that Saturday night, we'll be hosting the year's biggest banquet followed by the annual All-School All-Star Talent finals."

"Busy Saturday."

"*Nyes*. We hope to raise a good deal of money so we can send golf balls to our brave men and women serving overseas."

"Excuse me?" said Riley's mom.

"We're calling our gala celebration Greens for the Army Green. Tickets to the banquet and show will cost five hundred dollars apiece."

Riley nearly whistled, but he didn't want to earn an under-the-table shin kick from his mom.

"All proceeds will go toward sending golf equipment overseas to Afghanistan, which, if you ask me, is just one giant sand trap."

That was Mr. Paxton trying to make a joke.

"Um, my husband is serving over in Afghanistan."

"*Nyes*. So I heard. Chick Chambliss, head of country club security, has told me all about Colonel Richard Mack."

Riley's mom, who was decked out in her flowery Sunday-best dress, shot Riley a grin and a wink.

Mr. Paxton didn't realize that Chick Chambliss was Riley's godfather #24. When Riley was born, his dad had asked every guy in his unit to stand up for his son at the baptism, which took place at the base chapel over in Germany.

"I understand your husband is a decorated war hero?" said Mr. Paxton.

"He's won a few medals," said Riley, proudly.

"Well, Mrs. Mack, as I've said, I'd love for you and your son to be my guests at the banquet and for you to be one of the celebrity judges for the talent competition. General Joseph C. Clarke has already agreed to participate."

"But, Mr. Paxton, I'm not a celebrity."

"Poppycock. You're the wife of a war hero."

"Well, I'm not sure I . . ."

Mr. Paxton reached into his sport jacket and pulled out a thick envelope.

"To help you say yes, the Brookhaven Women's Auxiliary has put together a little package. There are coupons in here for hairstyling and a 'mani-pedi,' plus a one-thousand-dollar gift certificate from the Posh and Panache Dress Boutique on Main Street."

"Wow," said Riley. "Awesome swag, Mom."

"But, Mr. Paxton, I'm still not sure I'm qualified to judge talent . . ."

"Just follow Tony Peroni's lead."

"The wedding singer?"

"*Nyes.* He handles the preliminary rounds at the local schools."

"He's coming to Fairview Middle tomorrow," added Riley.

"Are you in the contest?" his mom asked.

"No way. But Briana is."

"Oh," said his mom, looking worried. "Is that okay? Briana Bloomfield is a family friend."

"That's fine," said Mr. Paxton, flashing his toothy smile. "Ms. Bloomfield may not make it to the finals."

"Oh, she will," said Riley. "She's wicked talented."

"Is that so? Well, it won't really matter if your young friend is one of the contestants, Mrs. Mack. The show's all done in good fun."

"Um, I thought the winner got, like, a ginormous college scholarship," said Riley, because Briana had told him she "really, really" needed to make it to the finals and win because her earthy-crunchy parents weren't what anybody would call rich. Without the All-School All-Star Talent Scholarship (and a few others), Briana Bloomfield would have an extremely hard time paying for college.

"*Nyes*. That's right. I believe there's a ten-thousand-dollar grand prize."

This time, Riley *did* whistle.

He also felt his cell phone vibrating in his pocket.

"Well, Mr. Paxton, I'd be honored . . ."

While his mom and Mr. Paxton went over the details of her judging duties, Riley slipped his smartphone out of his pocket and checked the text that had just come in from Briana Bloomfield.

EMERGENCY! S.P. PLANNING TALENT SHOW SABO-TAGE!!!

Riley quickly tapped out a reply.

PP 2 P.M. ROUND UP THE GANG.

PP was short for the Pizza Palace, the spot on Main Street where Riley and his crew always met to strategize.

S.P. was Briana's abbreviation for Sara Paxton—the meanest girl ever to attend Fairview Middle School.

Sara was also the daughter of the country club president—the man sitting across the table from Riley eating booger-covered eggs.

A LITTLE BEFORE 2:00 P.M., Riley and his good friend Mongo biked over to Main Street to meet up with Briana, Jake, and Jamal—Riley's whole crew—at the Pizza Palace.

Mongo's real name was Hubert Montgomery, but he was so gigantic (bigger and stronger than any seventh grader at any middle school anywhere in the known universe), everybody called him "Humongo" or Mongo for short. In fact, he was so huge that when he pedaled his bike, his knees came up to his chin.

"So what's the emergency again, Riley?"

Mongo also had trouble remembering stuff.

"Briana has uncovered a plot by Sara Paxton and her

gal pals to sabotage their competitors at the school talent show tomorrow."

"Is Sara the one who always calls me Butt Munch?"

"Yeah."

"She's pretty."

"Yeah," said Riley. "Pretty horrible."

Riley and Mongo locked their bikes to the rack outside the Pizza Palace and strode through the front door.

"Hi, guys," said Vinnie behind the counter. "The usual?"

"Sure," said Riley. Vinnie slapped one slice into the oven.

"You want a whole pie again, Mongo?"

"No thanks. I just ate lunch."

"How 'bout three slices of Meat Lover's, then?"

"Perfect!"

The guys paid and carried their greasy slices and cold drinks to the rear of the restaurant.

A wrinkled old lady was sitting in their usual booth.

Suddenly, the saggy-faced granny started waving at them, windmilling both her arms over her head. "Psst!" she hissed. "Riley! Mongo! It's me!"

Riley grinned. Briana Bloomfield was a master of all things theatrical, including disguises.

"Hurry up, you guys!" Briana was flapping her arms

at her sides now. "Sit down! This is so-o-o-o-o *horrific!*"

An extremely talented actress, Briana Bloomfield made everything she said come out with italics and exclamation points.

Riley scooted into the booth beside Briana. Mongo squeezed into the bench across from them. Tilting his head, he was staring at Briana the way a confused puppy stares at a human who says stuff it can't understand.

"Are you going to be a witch next year for Halloween?" Mongo asked.

"This? Nuh-unh. I was in my bedroom, practicing my old-age makeup in case I get cast in a summer stock production of *Arsenic and Old Lace* or something when school's out. Pretty awesome, huh? I did it with latex. You wad up crinkled Kleenex, then pour on the liquid plastic to make the wrinkles. And then I added in shadows and lines and junk with greasepaint, found the right wig, padded out this potato-sack dress, and voilà! I am *totally* a little old lady."

Mongo nodded like he understood.

"Dag, is that your grandmother, Riley Mack?"

Jamal Wilson, a wiry African American fifth grader, strolled up to the table. With extremely nimble fingers (which he used to do magic tricks and to crack open locks for fun), Jamal was the youngest and newest member of Riley's crew.

"It's me, Jamal!" whispered Briana.

"Really?" He scooted into the booth next to Mongo. "You need to stay out of the sun, girl. You've got more wrinkles than a box of raisins."

"It's my new makeup."

"Well, in that case, you need to go back to the store and demand a refund. Because—I'm just being honest here, Bree—your new makeup makes you look ancient, antiquated, and antediluvian."

Jamal also liked to memorize new words from the dictionary every day. Riley figured he had circled back to the *A*s.

"Do you know what those words mean?" Jamal asked Briana.

"Yep. Old."

"Sorry I'm late, guys." Jake Lowenstein, his hands stuffed inside the front pocket of his dragon-print hoodie, shuffled up to the table. "Mr. Holtz asked me to swing by school and help him wire things up in the auditorium for tomorrow's talent show. He never remembers how the microphones work. Or the light board."

Jake, who was the crew's technogeek–slash–electronics-and-computer wizard, scooched into the booth next to Riley.

"So what's up with Sara Paxton?" Riley asked, now

that his team was fully assembled. "Is she really trying to bump you out of the competition by sabotaging your act?"

"Not *me*," said Briana. "This is way worse. Sara, Brooke, and Kaylie are out to crush the fifth graders!"

"Which ones?" demanded Jamal, the only fifth grader currently seated at the table.

"Staci Evans and that bunch. Six of them are doing this dynamite roller-skating act that's absolutely *fabtastic*! I saw them rehearsing it on Friday."

Jamal nodded. "I helped choreograph a few of their smoother moves."

"So what makes you think Sara wants to sabotage the roller skaters?" asked Riley.

"Okay, this is way weird. I was in my bedroom, working on my makeup like I said, when I got this text. From Sara!"

"Interesting."

"Yuh-hunh. I figure it was a mistake because I'm still in her phonebook or whatever."

Riley knew that, last year, in the sixth grade, Briana had been Sara Paxton's "fourth musketeer." But, the instant seventh grade started, Queen Bee Sara and her two other "best friends forever," Brooke Newton and Kaylie Holland, had turned on Briana and made *her* their primary target.

"So, what'd the text say?" asked Jake, pushing his

glasses up the bridge of his nose.

"Hang on," said Briana as she pulled her iPhone out of the baggy hip pocket of her granny dress: "'MEET ME AT SKATE TOWN. NOW! IT'S TIME FOR OUR COMPETITION TO HAVE AN ACCIDENT.'"

"SO, ANYWAY," SAID BRIANA, **"SINCE** I was already in disguise and everything, I decided to head over to Skate Town and spy on them!"

Skate Town was a small shop on Main Street that specialized in skates and skating gear. Roller skates, rollerblades, and skateboards in the warm months; hockey skates and figure skates in the cold ones.

"What'd you find out?" asked Riley.

"Two things. One: this is an absolutely amazeriffic disguise. Nobody knew I was even in the store. I spent most of my time flipping through Spandex pants on a circular rack. Two: Sara, Brooke, and Kaylie were *totally* flirting with Disco Dan, the high school dude behind the counter—you know, the one who never buttons the top three buttons of his shiny shirt?"

"Did you hear what they were talking about?"

"Nun-unh. Just a bunch of giggles from the girls and 'Right on!' from Disco Dan. He is *so-o-o-o* stuck in the seventies. His hair is sproingier than a full-blown Chia Pet. And who wears purple-tinted sunglasses—*indoors*?"

"Okay," said Riley. "We need to check this out. Jake? How late is Skate Town open?"

"Hang on." Jake swiped his fingers across the glass face of his smartphone. "According to their website, they're 'open Sundays till six.'"

"Excellent. It's time to put together our countersabotage response."

Mongo raised his hand. "Um, Riley, don't we have to figure out what Sara and the mean girls are going to do before we can stop them from doing it?"

"Exactly."

"Well, whatever it is," said Jamal, "I'm sure it is foul and heinous. You know what that means?"

Riley just shrugged because he knew Jamal would tell him.

"It means Sara Paxton and her associates are up to some kind of chicanery. You know what *chicanery* means?"

"The same thing as heinous?" said Mongo.

"No! *Chicanery* means 'dirty tricks'! Sara Paxton and her posse are attempting to steal this talent competition from people with talent!"

"Which would be everybody except them," said Briana.

"Okay, Briana?" said Riley. "Head home. Get out of your costume and makeup. We may need some voice work this afternoon."

"Who am I gonna pretend to be this time?"

"Don't know yet. Jake? Take Jamal over to your house, get things up and running in the basement."

"No problem. My parents are both at their offices."

"Sweet. Mongo?"

"Yeah?"

"You and me are heading down to Skate Town to run a reconnaissance mission."

"What am I supposed to do?"

"Look big and strong."

"Oh. Okay. I can do that."

Riley glanced at his watch. "It's two fifteen now. Let's reconvene at Jake's place at three thirty."

"We must cause this heinous chicanery to cease!" said Jamal.

Riley shrugged again. "Works for me."

Riley and Mongo hurried up the street, past the diner and Mister Guy's Pet Supplies.

"You know," said Mongo, "I didn't think we'd be so busy this week, seeing how it's the last week of school and all. I was kind of hoping we could spend our afternoons chilling up at Schuyler's Pond. It's so hot out already."

"We'll get there, big guy. But right now, we need to fight for truth, justice, and the American way."

"Isn't Superman supposed to do that?"

"Yeah. But even Superman can't be everywhere at once."

"True. Especially now. I hear he's making a new movie."

Riley and Mongo reached Skate Town and stepped into the store.

The walls were covered with shelves of rainbow-colored roller skates. Disco music was thumping out of ceiling speakers. A rotating mirror ball swirled tiny squares of reflected light around the room. It was like walking inside a pinball machine from 1979.

"Keep the funk rollin'!" shouted Disco Dan, the shopkeeper. He was maybe seventeen and had to shout to be heard over the music: a woman singing about skating straight into somebody's heart, which sounded kind of messy to Riley.

"That's Daphne Champlain," said Disco Dan, grooving to the beat.

"Who?" said Riley.

Disco Dan rhythmically (and repeatedly) pointed to an album cover hanging on the wall in a sparkling gold frame. The woman on the cover was an African American with long curly hair.

"Daphne 'The Roller Disco Queen' Champlain." He jabbed a finger toward the ceiling (over and over) while shouting, "Whoop! Whoop!"

"We need to ask you a few questions," said Riley.

"Be right with you, cats. Whoop whoop!"

Riley turned to Mongo and raised one eyebrow.

Mongo nodded.

"We need to ask our questions *now*!" boomed Mongo.

Disco Dan lowered his dark-purple shades so he could see who was yelling at him. When he saw it was a guy the size of a refrigerator, his disco finger slid down to turn off the disco music.

"Dyn-o-mite. What's happenin', man?"

"We're looking for Sara Paxton, Brooke Newton, and Kaylie Holland," said Riley. "They're all blond. Twelve years old. Kind of look like matching Barbie dolls?"

"I can dig it. Three little ladies matching that description were in here a couple hours ago."

"What'd they want?" blurted Mongo.

"To check out my mondo cool moves. Whoop! Whoop!"

"What else?"

"Sorry, little brother. Chicks that groovy? They are out of your league."

Riley looked to Mongo.

Mongo stepped forward. Leaned in. Let Disco Dan smell his pizza breath.

"What. Else?"

Disco Dan shot up his hands. "The young ladies were also interested in a little righteous skate maintenance tip from yours truly."

"What did they want to know?" asked Riley.

"How they could loosen the front wheels so they could, you know, oil the ball bearings. I showed them how it's done. Of course, the most important part is making sure you tighten up that axle nut when you put the wheels back on."

"How come?"

"You don't tighten that sucker right, the wheel will come flying off in the middle of your roller disco routine."

"IT'S A CHEAP AND DIRTY trick straight out of Roller Derby," said Riley.

"If the wheels fall off the front axle," said Jake as he studied an exploded-parts view of a typical quad skate on his computer screen, "then the toe-stop at the tip will drop down and dig into the floor. It'll be like slamming on the skate's brakes."

"Making the fifth graders fall flat on their faces," added Riley.

"I guess beating a few fifth graders isn't enough for Sara Paxton," said Jamal. "She wants to humiliate them, too!"

"And break their noses," added Mongo.

Riley and his crew were down in the wood-paneled rumpus room where Jake kept his twelve computers (eight of which he had built himself), all sorts of tweaked-out electronic gear, and, of course, Riley's favorite piece of low-tech equipment, the foosball table.

"Riley?" said Briana. "We need to *do* something!"

"Bree's right," said Jamal. "We need to sabotage their sabotage!"

Mongo raised his hand.

"Yes?" said Riley.

"Are these roller skating fifth graders good?"

"They're *fantabulous*," gushed Briana.

"Well," said Mongo, kind of meekly, "what if we protect them and they end up winning the talent show and you don't get that college scholarship you need so much?"

"Mongo, I don't want to win by cheating. I want to win by *singing*!" Briana slowly sang some sad lines from "Hallelujah," that song from *Shrek*.

Riley thought it was, to borrow Briana's word, fabtastic.

"If you could sing like that while roller skating," said Jamal, "you'd win for sure, girl."

Briana acted appalled. "I am not cheating nor will I be stealing the Rockin' Rollers synchronized skating idea. I intend to win this competition, and the finals at the country club, fair and square."

"Works for me," said Riley.

"So what're we gonna do?" asked Mongo.

"A little plan I call Operation Roller Disco. Jamal?"

"Yeah?"

"Do you know the fifth graders doing the roller skating bit?"

"Sure. I, much like you, Riley Mack, strive to make friends with everyone I meet."

"Good. Reach out to the kids in the skate troupe. Tell them, no matter what, they are not to let their skates out of their sight tomorrow. They should keep them locked up till the show starts at two p.m."

"Um, okay," said Jamal. "But, that's it? I'm telling folks to keep an eye on their personal belongings?"

"That's it."

"Okay, but if you ask me, it doesn't sound like much of a caper. In fact, this operation is so simple, it probably doesn't even deserve its own name."

Riley grinned. "That's it—*for you*."

"Oh," said Jamal, nodding knowingly. "There's *more*."

"Isn't there always?" said Briana, making *gimme* gestures with both hands. "Come on, Riley. What else?"

"Jake? Can you gain early access to the backstage area?"

"Sure. Mr. Holtz wants me there an hour before the show starts. I guess this Tony Peroni, the judge, is a major recording star."

"Oh, he is!" said Briana. "His song 'Make Me Merry, Mary—Marry Me!' was a huge hit back in the eighties! He still makes a ton of money from its royalties. That's how he funds the All-School All-Star Talent Scholarship."

"And because he 'truly and sincerely loves to perform,'" added Jake, who had already run a Google search on Tony Peroni, "he also does a lot of weddings. Especially at the Brookhaven Country Club."

"I like weddings," said Mongo. "Weddings always have cake."

Riley grabbed a sheet of paper and a marker and drew a quick sketch of the middle-school stage.

"Okay. This is the curtain. Over here, in the stage left wings, the band usually leaves a bunch of junk. Music stands. Kettledrums. Over here, stage right, we have the cubicle that the music teacher, Mrs. Yasner, uses for her office. Briana—where will the acts be waiting before they go on?"

"We're supposed to get dressed in the bathrooms or the locker rooms and then use Mrs. Yasner's office as the greenroom."

"Is her office painted green?" asked Mongo.

"Um, no. The greenroom is what theater people call the place where performers wait."

"I knew that," said Jamal.

"Jake?" said Riley.

"Yeah?"

"I want you to set up miniature surveillance cameras *here* and *here*."

"I'll go with the five-point-eight–gigahertz wireless spy cam with the USB adapter so we can beam the images directly to my laptop."

"Cool." Riley circled the area in front of Mrs. Yasner's office. "We'll put six pairs of roller skates right here, forty minutes before show time."

"Yo, Riley Mack?" said Jamal. "I thought I was supposed to tell Staci and that bunch to keep their skates in their lockers?"

"You are."

"So whose skates are we gonna put outside the greenroom?"

"The ones Disco Dan is going to donate for the talent show."

"Huh?"

Riley turned to Briana. "You ever heard of a Roller Disco Queen named Daphne Champlain?"

"Sure. She had all sorts of big hits. 'Skate Scat Boogie,' 'It's a Heart Skate,' 'Skate School.'"

"Can you sound like her?"

"Riley, puh-leeze. Give me an hour and I can sound like anybody!"

"Excellent. Jake—pull up all the Daphne Champlain sound clips you can find on the internet."

"On it."

Riley glanced at his watch. "Okay. It's almost four. I want Daphne Champlain calling Skate Town by five so her grandson can go pick up the skates before the shop closes at six."

"Wha-huh?" said Briana.

"That's the scam. You're Daphne Champlain. You call Disco Dan."

"I can rig it so the caller ID on the Skate Shop end reads 'D. Champlain,'" said Jake.

"Perfect. Briana, you tell Disco Dan that your grandson goes to Fairview Middle School. At the last minute, he calls you out in Hollywood to say he's in this talent show tomorrow and that he and his five friends all need roller skates, so it would mean the world to you, Daphne Champlain, if Disco Dan could let the kids borrow six pairs for one day."

"Riley Mack?" said Jamal. "Not to pooh-pooh your plan, but I note one serious flaw: How are we gonna get Daphne Champlain's grandson to head over to Skate Town before six o'clock when we don't even know if she *has* a grandson or where he lives?"

"Easy," said Riley. "*You're* him."

THE CALL WENT OFF WITHOUT a hitch.

Briana totally nailed Daphne Champlain's voice. Disco Dan couldn't wait to meet her grandson and donate the skates.

Jamal went to Skate Town a little before six. Mongo went with him (but didn't go into the store) to help carry the heavy boxes back to Jake's house.

While he was in Skate Town, Jamal even signed an autograph.

"I told him my name was Daffy," he reported. "Daffy Champlain. Because I was named after my grammy, who, Disco Dan reminded me, won three Grammy Awards. That young man is seriously whacked, ya'all. I think disco fever fried a few of his brain cells."

"Okay, Jamal—new assignment: Tomorrow, at school, get within earshot of Sara, Brooke, or Kaylie and make a big stink about how you're working with the fifth-grade roller skaters. Say, you're their equipment manager."

"Do I need a costume? Maybe a jaunty cap?"

"Nope. Just make sure at least one of the mean girls hears you talking about how you need to set up the roller skates outside the greenroom thirty minutes before the show starts."

"No problem. I am very good at being loquacious and/or garrulous. Do you know what that means?"

"Yeah," said Briana. "You blab a lot."

"Indeed I do, Briana. Indeed I do."

"Okay," said Riley, "it's nearly seven. I have to head home."

"Are you chatting with your dad tonight?" asked Mongo.

Riley smiled. "Right after dinner."

"Awesome," said Briana. "I guess I better head home and put together my own costume for the talent show."

Mongo's moony face lit up. "Are you going to dress like Shrek when you sing 'Hallelujah'?"

"Um, no. That would be stupidious."

"Princess Fiona?"

"No, Mongo. My mom made me this really pretty

34

white dress so I'll glow like an angel when the spotlight hits me!"

"I hope you win," said Jake.

"Thanks. I just hope I do a good job and don't forget my lyrics!"

"Oh, yeah," said Jamal. "You do that, you're toast. I have seen what they do to singers who blow the lyrics on *American Idol* and, trust me, girl: It is *not* pretty."

Everybody headed home.

Riley was feeling pretty good, the way he always did after he saw a wrong and figured out how to make it right.

He felt even better when he linked up with his dad for a laptop chat.

Riley's father, Colonel Richard Mack (who everybody called Mack) was currently overseas with the Special Forces in Afghanistan. Thanks to Skype, Riley and his dad could still talk two or three times a week—chatting across several thousand miles and nearly as many time zones.

"Your mom is superexcited about this charity thing at the country club," his dad said.

"Yeah. It's going to be extremely fancy. They're charging five hundred dollars a ticket!"

Riley's dad whistled.

"I just hope they don't make us eat eggs Benedict."

His father laughed. "Don't worry, son. It's a banquet. You'll probably have some kind of rubbery chicken."

"Do they put yellow goop on it?"

"Negative. Chicken goop is typically brown."

"Cool."

"It was awfully nice of Mr. Paxton to invite your mother to be a VIP."

"Yeah. He's pretty decent, I guess. But . . ."

His father arched an eyebrow. "But what?"

"Well, his daughter, Sara, she's in this big talent contest tomorrow at school and we found out she's trying to eliminate her competition by, basically, taking them out of the game."

"How so?"

"We uncovered intelligence suggesting she and her accomplices will be tampering with some fifth graders' roller skates to make the wheels fall off in the middle of their act."

"Have you shared this information with the proper authorities?"

"No. Not yet. But, well, Sara Paxton is superpopular at school. Not just with the kids, but the teachers and the principal, too. She's a cheerleader and president of every club. It would just be my word against hers and her word would definitely win."

"Can you take independent action to thwart Ms. Paxton's efforts without causing physical injury to her and/or school property?"

"Yeah. I think so. And, if we don't, those fifth graders will be the ones getting physically injured."

"Then do what's right, son. Defend those who can't defend themselves."

"I'll try."

"Good. May I make one request?"

"Sure."

"Let's keep your mother out of the loop on all things Paxton. We don't want anything to ruin her big night at the country club."

"Gotcha. No problem."

Riley and his father spent another half hour chatting about all kinds of stuff. His father told Riley how he and his men were spending some time doing humanitarian visits to Afghan hospitals and teaching the locals how to play baseball. Then, right before they signed off, Riley's dad said something that gave Riley a huge lump in his throat.

"Son, I am delighted to see you using your extraordinary talents to serve a cause greater than yourself. Keep up the good work!"

Of course, Riley and his dad both knew that Riley Mack hadn't *always* used his "extraordinary talents" to do good.

Three years ago, a few days before Riley's ninth

birthday, his dad received new orders and shipped out to a far-off combat zone, meaning he wouldn't be around to celebrate Riley's big day with ice cream and cake.

First, that made Riley sad. Next, it made him mad. Then, he did something extremely bad.

On the morning of his ninth birthday, Riley went to the supermarket and stole a whole ice-cream cake, which he stuffed down the front of his pants. Riley had always been clever. Cunning. But that day, he was actually kind of stupid.

First of all, an ice-cream cake is a pretty huge thing to smuggle out of a store inside your pants. Second, the ice cream melted quickly, so wherever Riley walked, he dribbled an easy-to-follow trail of milky goo. He was busted before he made it past the bag boys.

He and his dad had a long, long talk on their laptops that night.

Surprisingly, his father didn't yell or scream. Didn't threaten to have Riley's mom take away all his video games or lock him in his room till he turned eighteen. In fact, his father remained eerily calm.

"Son," he said, his voice strong and firm, "as you know, because of my commitment to our country, I cannot be there to babysit you twenty-four/seven. Therefore, you have a choice. You can keep acting up, being selfish, causing your mother grief. Or you can use your incredible skills and talents to serve some-thing bigger than yourself. Your choice, son. I suggest you choose wisely."

That's why Riley had a lump in his throat.

His father had just told him he'd chosen wisely.

PRESCOTT PAXTON FINISHED UP HIS overseas phone call.

"There's no more left in the field?"

"None that we know of, sir," said his subordinate. "The recall worked quietly and efficiently. And your follow-up notion was sheer brilliance."

That made Paxton smile. Of course it was brilliant. Everything Prescott P. Paxton did was a stroke of genius. That's how he had become chairman and CEO of Xylodyne Dynamics.

"Excellent work over there, Crumpler."

"Thank you, Mr. Paxton. I feel we can press forward on the project with confidence. If there's any further push-back on this side, I've set up a contingency plan."

"Ah! Thinking ahead, eh?"

"Yes, sir."

"Remind me to put you down for a bonus, Crumpler."

"Yes, sir, Mr. Paxton. I sure will."

Paxton glanced at his sparkling Rolex watch.

"Need to run. My daughter is in a talent contest at her school this afternoon."

"I hope she wins, sir."

"*Nyes.* I'm sure she will."

On the drive over to Fairview Middle School in his sleek Mercedes, Paxton contemplated his next moves.

Potential disaster had been averted. It was, indeed, time to move forward and land the next big fish.

His multinational corporation, Xylodyne, did billions of dollars' worth of business with the United States military and had all sorts of contracts to supply goods and services to troops stationed overseas.

It was time to pick up a few more.

That was the real reason behind the whole Greens for the Army Green gala at the country club. Frankly, he couldn't care less about sending golf balls to the "brave men and women" in the military.

In fact, the very notion made Paxton laugh.

Everybody knew that people only joined the army

when they couldn't find a real job, like being chairman and CEO of Xylodyne Dynamics. But, he'd keep those kinds of thoughts to himself. He'd pretend to be patriotic and slap magnetic yellow ribbons on the bumpers of all the country club's golf carts.

Inviting the local war hero's wife to the banquet and talent show finals was yet another stroke of Paxton genius. The Pentagon general he was also inviting would be impressed and eager to do more business with a patriotic, army-wife-supporting chairman and CEO such as Prescott P. Paxton.

As he cruised down a leaf-dappled lane, he said to his steering wheel, "Call office!" A hands-free speakerphone dial-toned, then diddled out the digits.

His secretary picked up on the second ring.

"Xylodyne Dynamics. Mr. Paxton's office."

"*Nyes*, Ginger, it's me."

"Yes, sir, Mr. Paxton. Did your daughter win the talent contest?"

"Not yet. But I'm sure she will. Did we hear back from General Clarke?"

"Yes, sir. He'd be delighted to join you at Brookhaven for the gala and has agreed to serve as a judge."

"Wonderful!" Paxton's day just kept getting better and better.

"And sir, may I just say that my husband and I had brunch at the country club yesterday, and the landscaping renovations look spectacular! The greens are so lush and, well, green!"

"*Nyes*, they certainly are. I'll be at Fairview Middle School till three. If there's an emergency, you know how to reach me."

"Yes, sir."

"End call."

The speakerphone did as it was told. Paxton liked appliances that obeyed him.

When the golf course was reopened, Paxton felt certain the membership would vote to have his historic term as club president commemorated on a plaque of some sort. Maybe they'd even ask him to sit for a portrait to hang on the Wall of Esteemed Past Presidents.

He had been president of Brookhaven for two years, and the relandscaped golf course would be his legacy. Work had started late last fall and, even though it had cost a fortune, continued throughout the winter and into the spring. Now the course was less than two weeks away from reopening.

Paxton pulled into the middle school's parking lot. As instructed, the assistant principal, Mr. Ball, had blocked off the one remaining visitor parking slot at the front of the school with a bright orange traffic cone, reserving it for Prescott P. Paxton.

Of course he had.

Mr. Ball and his wife enjoyed receiving reduced

"scholar's rate" memberships at the Brookhaven Country Club, a discount that could only be approved by the current club president.

It's good to be king, Prescott thought proudly.

And then he entered the school to watch his princess, Sara, win the talent-competition crown.

RILEY AND JAKE CROUCHED BEHIND the kettledrums on the left hand side of the stage.

"Video signal is coming in four-by-four," whispered Jake, angling his laptop screen so both he and Riley could see the two spy cam shots of the roller skates lined up in front of Mrs. Yasner's office cubicle.

"Four by four" meant the signal was strong and clear.

Riley glanced at his watch: 2:40 p.m. Twenty minutes till showtime.

He was about to mutter, "Where are they?" when Jake tapped him on the shoulder.

Across the stage, a door creaked open.

Sara Paxton, Brooke Newton, and Kaylie Holland

came tiptoeing up the steps to the stage right wings.

"Shhh! Be quiet, you guys," said Sara.

All three girls were wearing spangly baseball caps perched sideways atop their golden hair and some kind of red-white-and-blue sequined leotards.

"Get out your wrenches, girls!" whispered Sara.

Riley and Jake watched as the girls fiddled with the front axle nuts on all six pairs of skates lined up outside Mrs. Yasner's office. The digital recorder in the laptop captured their every move.

"Okay," said Sara. "Let's go. We need to rehearse some more."

"What?" whined Brooke. "We already rehearsed, like, two times."

"Chya!" agreed Kaylie.

"I don't care," said Sara, planting a hand firmly on her hip. "We need to win. If we don't, my daddy will be very, very disappointed."

Kaylie and Brooke shivered with dread and the three of them scurried off the stage.

"We got 'em!" said Riley.

"Maybe we should grab a pair of skates and have Ms. Kaminski dust them for fingerprints," suggested Jake.

Ms. Mary Kaminski was a young science teacher at Fairview Middle School who was a total CSI freak. She had even started an after-school club called CSI:

Middle School Edition. Science experiments in her class sometimes involved cool stuff like fingerprinting and tomato splatter patterns.

"Good idea, Jake," said Riley. "But I think our video clip is all the forensic evidence we need."

"Should we take it to the principal's office?"

"Let's wait till after the show. I want to see Sara's face when the fifth graders roll onstage and their wheels don't fly off."

Jake closed the laptop and tucked it under his arm.

"There you are!"

It was Mr. Holtz, the teacher who everybody thought knew everything about the school's AV and computer equipment. Actually, all he knew was how to find Jake Lowenstein.

"Hey, Mr. Holtz," said Jake, passing the laptop off to Riley. "What's up?"

"This Saturday? Are you busy?"

"Well . . ."

"Because there's a two o'clock wedding reception at the country club. I just bumped into Tony Peroni out in the hall. His usual sound guy is out of town, so he asked me to run his sound system for that, too!"

Riley smiled.

That meant Mr. Holtz had to ask Jake to run it—if anybody wanted it to run properly.

"I'll pay you ten bucks."

"That's okay, Mr. Holtz," said Jake. "I do it for the challenge."

"It should be a simple setup. Just Peroni and his electric-keyboard player, Greg Wu. Ooh. Here's Mr. Peroni now!"

A chubby man in a tuxedo with a ruffled shirt waddled through the stage door. His swept-back pouf of hair looked like it used to be jet-black. Now it was *dyed* jet-black (except for the white roots). It looked like Mr. Peroni shampooed with liquid shoe polish.

"Mr. Peroni?" called the teacher. "This is Jake Lowenstein. He's gonna help us out this Saturday for the wedding and next Saturday for the talent show finals."

"Beautiful, baby. Beautiful." When Tony Peroni thrust out his hand to shake with Jake, Riley caught a flash of diamonds from the wedding singer's horseshoe-shaped pinky ring. "How we looking here?"

"All set to go," said Mr. Holtz. "Right, Jake?"

Jake nodded.

Peroni nudged his head toward Riley. "You in the show, Red?"

"No, sir," said Riley. "Today, I'm just a guy in the audience enjoying the show."

"Beautiful, baby. Beautiful. Hey, Jack? Is it Jack?"

"No, sir. *Jake.*"

"Fantastic, kid, fantastic. Here's my CD. Cue up track

48

one. It's my killer opener. Who's running the follow-spot?"

Mr. Holtz raised his hand.

"Terrific, baby. Just keep it locked on *me* whenever I'm onstage."

Riley could hear the audience starting to assemble on the other side of the red velvet curtain.

He stepped away from Jake, Mr. Holtz, and Tony Peroni so he could tap the Motorola H9 Bluetooth Headset jammed deep in his left ear. The thing was about the size of a dime and allowed you to listen and talk on your cell without anybody knowing. Jake's dad had boxes of them stored on a shelf outside the furnace room. He did some kind of supersecret work for the government and people were forever sending him gizmos and gadgets. Riley and his crew made sure none of the stuff ever went to waste.

"Jamal?"

"Standing by, Riley Mack."

"You did good. The girls took the bait. We have them on video. How's Briana?"

"Nervous and anxious. She's down in the girls' locker room putting on her costume."

"She's gonna win this thing fair and square!"

"That's Mongo," said Jamal. "I was showing him how to work his Bluetooth."

"It's so small," said Mongo, "it could fit in my nose. But, then, I wouldn't be able to hear you guys. Would I?"

Riley grinned. "All right, everybody. Head to the auditorium. It's time to sit back, relax, and enjoy the show!"

"Mr. Mack?"

Riley spun around.

It was Assistant Principal Ball.

"Did you know," he said, "that Disney doesn't have an 'Education Channel'?"

"No, sir," Riley said breezily. "Then again, I don't watch too much TV. Not when I've got homework to do."

The assistant principal squinted. He didn't like Riley. Never had. Probably never would.

"What, may I ask, are you doing in the backstage area? Are you part of this afternoon's entertainment?"

"Not right now, sir. But, maybe after school, if you're free." He tapped the laptop he had tucked under his arm. "I just found this hilarious little video that I think you're gonna love!"

RILEY AND MONGO TOOK THEIR usual seats at the rear of the auditorium.

(The back row was the easiest to slip out of whenever duty called. It was also the best place to take a snooze if the assembly was boring.)

Jamal was seated down near the front, with the rest of the fifth graders.

Assistant Principal Ball was at center stage, in front of the red curtain, tapping a microphone.

"Is this thing on?"

"Yes, Principal Ball!" said the entire auditorium.

"Good. Well, boys and girls, welcome to the last week of school."

Mr. Ball looked surprised when the audience erupted with applause, *booyahs*, shouts of joy, and some scattered chants of "USA! USA!"

Assistant Principal Ball raised two fingers, the school's universal signal for everyone to be quiet or wind up in detention hall. It was extremely kindergarten, but it worked.

"Now, as a special end-of-the-school-year treat, I want to bring on a very famous singer, the one and only Tony Peroni."

The crowd went wild.

Tony Peroni, bathed in a bright white circle of light, sashayed onto the stage, snapping his fingers.

"Hit it, Jack!"

And he still couldn't remember Jake's name.

Jazzy music featuring a ton of trombones, sizzling cymbals, and a plinking piano boomed from the speakers.

Riley figured it was track one from the CD.

On the downbeat, Peroni crooned, "Make me merry, Mary, say you'll marry me. Make me merry, Mary. C'mon and marry me."

Fortunately, Mr. Peroni didn't sing too much more. The lyrics kind of repeated themselves.

"Thank you, ladies and gentlemen, boys and girls. It's a special thrill and honor for me to be here at . . ."

Peroni glanced at the inside of his palm.

". . . Fairview Middle School. You know, that little ditty, 'Make Me Merry, Mary—Marry Me!' has certainly made me a merry man. A number-one hit back in the late eighties, and still available on iTunes, it has made me so much money, well, I'm always looking to give a little back. To encourage kids to use their talents and follow their dreams. That's why I set up the All-School All-Star Talent Scholarship fund!"

The audience applauded.

"Thank you. Sincerely. I mean it. From the bottom of my heart. Last year, we did the high schools. Next year, we're hittin' the elementary schools. This year? Well, you beautiful middle schoolers, it's your turn! And, dig this: the finals will take place at the Brookhaven Country Club. Beautiful venue. Love what they've done with their lawn. The top talents from all three middle schools in the district will compete for the grand prize—a ten-thousand-dollar college scholarship!"

More applause and a couple *whoo-hoo*s, mostly from Mongo.

"Okay. Here are the rules. Today, by listening to *your* applause, I will pick one singing act and one other act to move forward to the finals. Later this week, I'll host competitions at the other two middle schools until we have our six finalists. And, since it's *my* scholarship, I can also pick one wild-card contestant, an act I

53

personally think deserves a shot at the crown, even if you kids don't clap for 'em!"

Riley wondered if Peroni would use his "wild card" to bump Sara Paxton up to the finals after Briana won the applause-o-meter contest. After all, he seemed to work a lot at Sara's father's country club.

"But hey, school's almost out for the summer," Peroni continued. "Enough with the rules. Let's get this show on the road, baby!"

The audience screamed in agreement.

Peroni reached into his tux pocket and pulled out a note card.

"First up, from the seventh grade, singing and tap-dancing to 'America the Beautiful,' let's give it up for three American beauties—Sara Paxton and her Star-Spangled Starlettes!"

The three girls, looking like an American flag made out of reflectors, jumped around the stage as if they were doing a cheerleading routine. They also shook red-white-and-blue Mylar pom-poms. They sang okay—if you enjoy hearing people shout lyrics while making choppy hand gestures to act out all the words (they pretended to pluck apples out of a tree for "above the fruited plain").

But it was a patriotic song. Sara, Kaylie, and Brooke had all sorts of energy and did a flashy finish where they jumped into a full split and tossed their sparkling baseball caps up into the air.

The audience gave them a ton of applause, so they definitely had a shot.

Until people hear Briana sing, Riley thought.

Sara and her crew hurried offstage—squealing, clapping, and doing cheerleader kicks. They took seats down in the front row so they could watch the other acts.

"Okay," said Tony Peroni. "Beautiful. God bless America. I mean that. Sincerely. Next up, from the fifth grade, the Rockin' Rollers!"

Riley craned his neck so he could check out Sara Paxton's reaction as the six daredevil fifth graders skated onto the stage and started rolling through their incredible jumps, spins, leaps, and stunts—*without* their wheels flying off.

Surprisingly, Sara didn't seem shocked at all.

In fact, she was clapping and pumping her arm in time to their music.

So were Brooke and Kaylie.

"This is bad," mumbled Riley.

"Really? I think they're pretty good," said Mongo.

Riley could see Jamal down with the fifth graders. He whipped around with a panicked *what's going on?* look on his face.

All Riley could do was shrug.

And applaud with the rest of the audience when the

skaters finished their awesome act.

"Wow," said Tony Peroni. "That was incredible! I mean that. Sincerely. That's the act to beat, boys and girls!"

The fifth graders in the audience screamed for their classmates.

"And now, the song stylings of another seventh grader. The one and only Briana Bloomfield!"

Peroni gestured to the wings.

Nobody came onstage.

"Briana Bloomfield?"

Nothing.

Peroni fumbled with his note cards. "Is there a Briana Bloomfield in the house?"

That's when Jake, his head hanging low, plodded out from his sound tech station in the wings.

"Um," he mumbled, "Briana's not here."

"OKAY," SAID TONY PERONI. "BRIANA Bloomfield is a no-show."

The crowd gasped.

Except for Sara, Kaylie, and Brooke. They were giggling.

"We'll just scratch her from the competition," said Tony Peroni as he flipped through his note cards. "Let's move on to sixth grader Lenny Gonzalez, who's going to favor us with his fuzzbox version of the 'Iron Man' guitar solo."

As the guitar player rolled his amplifier onstage, Riley scooted up his row.

"'Scuse me. Coming through."

Mongo was right behind him.

They reached the aisle.

"Where are you boys going?" whispered Ms. Kaminski, the science teacher. She was supposed to supervise Riley's group of seventh graders in the auditorium during the assembly.

"We need to check on our friend," said Riley. "Briana must be sick. No way would she be a 'no-show.'"

"Go on," said Ms. Kaminski. "Hurry. When you find her, take her to the nurse's office!"

"Will do," whispered Riley. He and Mongo exited out the rear doors of the auditorium.

"Let's go check the greenroom," said Riley. "Maybe Briana's still back there."

They headed down the side corridor that led to the stage door.

"Why would she be in the greenroom?" asked Mongo.

"Maybe she got slammed with a bad case of stage fright."

"Briana?" said Mongo. "She's not afraid of anything."

Suddenly, Sara Paxton stepped out of the auditorium. She was grinning like the cat that had just eaten every bird in its backyard.

"Oh, hello, boys. Looking for your girlfriend?"

"We're looking for Briana!" said Mongo eagerly. "Do you know where she is?"

"Not really, Butt Munch. Maybe she had a wardrobe malfunction. Did you see that cheesy white dress her mother sewed together out of a tablecloth from Kmart or something? What is this, *Little House on the Prairie?*"

"Where is she, Sara?" demanded Riley.

Sara shrugged flippantly. "I dunno. All I know is where she *isn't*: onstage!"

"What'd you do?"

Sara flashed her shark-toothed smile. "Me? Um, excuse me, Riley. I think the better question is what did *you* and your stupid friends do?"

"Huh?" said Mongo, squinting hard.

"You texted Briana on purpose," said Riley, finally figuring it out. "You sent her that message to lure her into the skate shop."

"Well, duh," said Sara. "You think I would still have that gork's number in my phone book?" Sara made a few barfing sounds. "And then, of course, we had to wait for her to show up and, when she did, she was wearing that ridiculous granny costume. She smelled like mothballs."

Riley felt so stupid! They'd been set up.

"I knew you and your idiotic Gnat Pack would act all noble and heroic and cook up some kind of convoluted scheme to save the poor little fifth graders from mean ol' me. I knew you'd take your eyes off the real prize."

Of course, Riley thought.

Two acts from Fairview Middle School would move on to the finals: one singer, and one other act. Sara and her Star-Spangled Starlettes couldn't lose to the Rockin' Rollers. They could only lose to Briana or some other singer.

Sara smirked triumphantly. "Sorry, Riley. Game over. You lose."

"This isn't over, Sara."

"Um, yes it is. Because no way will I lose this competition to an ugly nobody from nowhere whose hippy-dippy parents are so beyond poor they couldn't even afford a real costume, not to mention all the private singing lessons and dance tutors and music coaches my daddy's bought for me."

"She has talent," said Riley. "It's all she needs."

"Oh, grow up, Riley Mack. There is absolutely no way that I will ever lose to a gork singing a sappy song from, gag me now, *Shrek*!"

"We'll see about that, Sara," said Riley, trying to muster a little of his cocky swagger. "Come on, Mongo."

Mongo's horror-filled eyes were the size of doughnuts. "Where are we going?"

"To find Briana."

Sara laughed. "Ha! Even if you two morons *do* find her, I guarantee you she will *not* be setting foot on that stage. If she does, she'll get expelled for 'indecent exposure.'"

Riley did not like the sound of that—or the look on Sara's face when she said it.

"Guess I better head back inside," Sara said with a fake sigh. "Tony Peroni will be announcing the winners in fifteen minutes and we got like a *ton* of applause from the audience! Too bad Briana won't be getting *any*!"

Sara turned on her heel and gave Riley and Mongo a bouncy little cheerleader kick as she dashed back into the auditorium.

"The girls' locker room!" said Riley, remembering where Jamal had said Briana was changing into her costume. "Come on, Mongo. If we hurry, we might be able to get Briana onstage before Tony Peroni announces the winners."

They jogged up the empty hallway toward the gym.

Ten seconds later, they both wished they hadn't.

Briana stumbled around a corner, tears streaming down her face.

She was clutching a towel wrapped around her otherwise naked body.

"They stole my clothes *and* my costume!" she cried. "Sara, Brooke, and Kaylie! They stole everything!"

RILEY COULD HEAR TONY PERONI'S amplified voice echoing up the hallway from the auditorium.

"The winners who will be representing Fairview Middle School at the All-School All-Star Talent Show in two weeks are: From the fifth grade, the Rockin' Rollers! And, from the seventh grade, Sara Paxton and her Star-Spangled Starlettes!"

The crowd cheered. A bell rang. School was done for the day.

So were Briana's chances of winning the scholarship.

Riley and Mongo were guarding the entrance to the girls' locker room.

"Hang on, Bree. Jamal and Jake are on the way."

Riley had sent the other two members of what Sara had called his Gnat Pack down to the costume storage room in the basement of the auditorium. Jake, who worked on the technical crews of every school play, knew where to find the wardrobe room. Jamal knew how to open any and all locks that stood in their way. Together, they would retrieve Briana's Maid Marian costume from last year's drama club production of *Robin Hood—The Musical*.

"Psst!" Briana whispered through the vent at the bottom of the locker room door. "Riley?"

"Yeah?"

"Did you and Jake catch Sara on video?"

"Yeah."

"Good! They are so busted. We should take the video to the office and . . ."

"I already thought about that. She played us, Bree. If we show the video, Sara will just claim that they were *tightening* the nuts on those axles to prevent the fifth graders from having an accident."

"That doesn't make sense," said Mongo. "They're mean girls."

"But the wheels didn't fly off. Nothing bad happened when the fifth graders rolled onstage. If we show Mr. Ball the video clip, he'll probably give Sara a safety medal to go with her talent show trophy!"

Riley heard a whimpering noise on the other side of the door.

Mongo knelt down and whispered through the vent. "Briana? Don't cry. Everything will turn out okay."

Jamal and Jake hustled up the hall with the Maid Marian costume.

"This is egregiously offensive, Riley Mack!" said Jamal. "Do you know what that means?"

"Yeah. It sucks."

Riley closed his eyes and knocked on the locker room door. "Okay, we have your costume. Jake texted your mom so you won't have to ride home on the bus."

The door creaked open an inch.

Riley passed Briana the dress.

"Thanks, you guys," said Briana. "Give me a second."

"Take all the time you need," said Riley as he, Mongo, Jake, and Jamal formed a human wall outside the door.

"So, Riley," whispered Jamal, "did Briana really hang with Sara and that bunch back in the day?"

Riley nodded.

"Was she mental?"

"What can I say? She was young."

"She was also, you know, confused," added Jake.

"Yeah," said Mongo. "I get that way sometimes, too. Especially during math class."

Riley remembered when he and Briana had first become friends. All through elementary school, Briana Bloomfield had hung out with Sara Paxton, Brooke Newton, and Kaylie Holland, who—according to everybody except Riley—were the coolest, prettiest, most popular girls in whatever school they attended.

But the minute seventh grade started, Briana's three "BFFLs" turned against her and started calling her Flaky Wakey and Gork Girl. Over the summer, the Mean Girls of Fairview Middle School had decided that they were way too mature to hang out with artsy-fartsy Briana Bloomfield.

Riley had known she would need new friends. So he became the first.

The locker room door opened. Briana stepped out in a puffy-sleeved, floor-length gown trimmed with fake fur and gold ribbons.

"Come, noble Sir Robin," she gushed to Riley, trying to hide her hurt under another make-believe character. "Wouldst thou and thy band of merry men kindly hie me hither to my mother's carriage?"

"That's from the show!" said Mongo.

"Um, not really. I'm kind of improvising here."

"You're good, girl," said Jamal. "It's like we're in Sherwood Forest—and I don't mean the subdivision out by the mall!"

Riley, Mongo, Jake, and Jamal created a box forma-
tion around Briana and walked her out of the building
to the parking lot.

"Thanks again, you guys, for finding my costume."

"No problem," said Jake.

"Did you want the pointy pink princess hat with the
streamer?" asked Jamal. "If so, I can . . ."

"Nope."

"Well, school's out in four days," said Jake, trying to
make Briana feel better.

"That's right," said Riley. "This time next week, we'll
all be swimming in Schuyler's Pond."

"Booyah!" said Mongo.

"Schuyler's Pond?" said Jamal, who hadn't been on
Riley's crew last summer. "Where's that?"

"It's our secret swimming hole," said Jake. "We
typically go there at least once a week, June through
August."

"Schuyler's Pond is so secret," added Mongo, "nobody
even knows it's there except my dad, who's the one
who told me about it. And, I guess Schuyler, whoever
he was. He probably knew about his pond, too."

"We'll go there," said Riley, who knew Briana needed
more than a pep talk. "After we make sure Briana is in
the talent show finals at the country club."

"Um, Riley—I totally missed the audition!"

"So?" said Riley, with a crafty twinkle in his eye. "I

have a funny feeling that you're going be Tony Peroni's wild-card pick."

"Really?" said Mongo. "How's that gonna happen?"

"I'm not sure. But, don't worry—I'm working on it."

THE LAST WEEK OF SCHOOL flew by in a blur.

Sara, Kaylie, and Brooke were still giggling at Riley, especially during lunch in the cafeteria. And on the school bus. And in homeroom.

Riley could not have cared less.

Because, by Wednesday, he had hatched his counterattack.

"I call it Operation Granny Smith," said Riley.

On Thursday night, his whole crew was assembled in Jake's basement, where their parents thought they were studying for the "*final* final" of the school year.

"Does your plan involve apples, Riley Mack?" asked Jamal. "If so, there are other varieties with much more

interesting names than Granny Smith. For instance—
Jonalicious, Geeveston Fanny, and Fukutami."

"Whoa," said Briana. "Have you switched from
memorizing the dictionary to memorizing the ency-
clopedia?"

"No. I have not 'switched.' I enjoy spending time with
both. Did I also mention that I've been working up a
new card trick this week?"

Jamal pulled out a deck of playing cards.

"Jamal?" said Riley. "Can we maybe check out the
new trick later? We've got work to do."

"Sure thing, Riley Mack. Yo, Jake. What's that in your
ear, man?"

Jake rolled his eyes as, once again, Jamal reached
into Jake's raised hood and came out with a quarter.

"Wow," said Mongo. "It's like Jake's head is a Coke
machine."

Riley just sighed. "Jake, roll out the floor plans."

"On it."

He cleared away a table covered with memory
boards, hard drives, capacitors, wire cutters, and sol-
dering irons so he could spread out several sheets of
paper that looked like blueprints.

"I printed out a blowup of the architectural schemat-
ics from the Brookhaven Country Club's most recent
renovations. The interior designers had the plans
posted on their website."

"The drawings are five years old," explained Riley, "but there have been no major changes to the layout in that time."

Riley tapped a large rectangle labeled THE CRANBROOK BALLROOM. "Okay, this is where the Smith–Oliverio wedding will be taking place on Saturday."

"The whoozeewhatsit?" said Briana.

"The wedding that Tony Peroni is singing at," said Jake.

Riley draped his arm over Jake's shoulder. "A wedding where our man Jake Lowenstein just happens to be on the technical crew."

"I'm just helping out Mr. Holtz."

"Which means we have an inside man."

"For what?" said Mongo.

"Briana's audition."

"Huh?" said Briana. "You expect me to audition for Tony Peroni in the middle of somebody else's wedding reception?"

Riley grinned. "No. At the start."

"Two p.m.," said Jake. "Sharp."

"You guys, no way is the wedding singer going to let me sing the first song at the reception."

"Oh, yes he will," said Riley. "Because you'll be saving his butt."

"Really? And how exactly am I going to do that?"

"With your karaoke machine. You still have it, right?"

"You bet," said Briana, excitedly. "Remember when I won it?"

Riley shot her a wink. "How could I forget? Jake?"

"Yeah?"

"Swing by Briana's house before Saturday. Pick up her karaoke box."

"How about tomorrow night?" suggested Briana. "You could stay for dinner. We're having tofu burgers. Again."

"Cool," said Jake. "It's a date."

When he realized what he'd just said, he gulped.

"I mean I'll be there."

"Excellent," said Riley. "While Jake sets up your karaoke machine inside the Cranbrook Ballroom, we need to get you into the club and up to the stage. How much cash do we have in the till?"

Mongo pulled open a file cabinet and checked out a mayonnaise jar stuffed with coins and wadded dollar bills.

"Five dollars and fifteen cents," he reported.

Riley reached into his jeans and pulled out a crinkled fifty-dollar bill. "Add in this."

"Whoa, Riley Mack," said Jamal. "That's your flash cash."

Riley had kept the fifty-dollar bill his grandparents sent him for Christmas two years ago. It was the money he pulled out whenever he needed to convince people that he had money.

"You can't put that in the jar, man," said Jamal.

"This is an emergency," said Riley, slipping his bill into the jar. "Briana needs to take a taxi to Brookhaven on Saturday so she looks like she belongs at the country club."

"That's never easy," said Jamal. "Trust me. Those snooty-patootie preppy types aren't big on drop-in visitors."

"Well, this is a wedding," said Riley. "The country club will be crawling with nonmembers. To blend in, you'll need to put on your old-age makeup again."

"Oh-kay," said Briana.

"You're Granny Smith. Which one is Smith again, Jake?"

Jake clacked a couple keys on his computer. "He's the groom."

"Right. You're the groom's grandmother. Nobody's going to stop a little old lady tottering down the hall with a corsage pinned to her chest. You'll need a different old-lady dress. Something blue, since you're with the groom."

Briana's eyes brightened. "I'll swing by the thrift shop. And I can make a corsage with flowers from my mom's garden and a glue gun."

"Excellent. I'll go in with you, Briana. In case anything goes wrong."

"You better wear a snappy jacket and tie," said Jamal.

"Don't worry, I've got one." Riley tugged at his collar, remembering how tight his tie had felt the last time he wore one. "I'll also need a box because I'm going in as a Smith kid—a niece or a nephew or a cousin. I'm lugging a huge wedding gift for my frail grandmother. The box needs to be big enough to hide my face in case Chick Chambliss is on duty."

"Who's this Chambliss character?" asked Jamal.

"Head of country club security. Used to be in my dad's outfit. Knows me. Knows my face."

"So we should find some shimmering silver paper and wrap up an empty cardboard crate from, like, a microwave oven!" said Briana.

Riley nodded. "I like it. We need to gain access to the club by one forty-five. Then, you duck into the ladies' powder room here." Riley tapped another box on the floor plan. "Where you change out of your granny getup."

"I could wear my real costume under my granny sack!" said Briana.

"Perfect," said Riley.

"But, um, what exactly am I going to sing?"

Riley turned to Jake. "Jake?"

"Well, according to their official wedding website, Casey Smith and Michele Oliverio list 'Colour My World' by Chicago as 'our song.'"

73

"Then that's what they'll want for their first dance," said Briana.

"Really?" said Jamal. "Are they old-school or what?"

"It's a classic. I already have the karaoke version in my machine."

"Good," said Riley. "See if you can dig up a sing-along disc of 'Make Me Merry, Mary—Marry Me!'"

"But that's Tony Peroni's big hit."

"I know. He'll need your help to sing it Saturday."

"Um, how come?"

"Because his piano player won't be showing up till *three*."

"Wait. You said the reception starts at two."

"Yeah. But we want to give the wedding guests the high-class entertainment first: the song stylings of Miss Briana Bloomfield. Besides, somebody's gonna call Tony Peroni's piano player with bum information about the start time."

"What? Who would do that?"

"Tony Peroni, himself," said Riley, with a wink. "Better known as Briana Bloomfield."

ON SATURDAY MORNING, RILEY, JAKE, and Briana were back in Jake's basement.

Riley's mom would be working at the bank all day. Jake's parents were both at their offices (again). Briana's mother and father encouraged her to "blossom wherever she was planted" so, basically, she didn't have all that much parental supervision most weekends.

"I've rigged up this phone to emulate the number Tony Peroni uses in his GigMasters listing on the web," explained Jake as he handed Briana a cell phone, which had a black wire dangling from it. "That acoustic coupler will feed your voice into this pitch modulator, so I can make your voice go deeper, to match Peroni's."

"You just have to concentrate on matching his style and pacing," said Riley.

Briana put the voice changer's headphone over one ear and held the phone up to the other. "You mean like this, baby. Perfect. Beautiful. Sincerely. I mean that."

"Awesome," said Riley. "Jake, place the call."

"What's the piano player's name again?" asked Briana.

"Greg Wu."

"Got it." Briana held up her hand to let the guys know the call had rung through. "Greggy, baby? Yeah. Tony. Beautiful. Slight change of plans this afternoon. Right. The wedding gig at Brookhaven Country Club. Seems the groom wanted to catch a little extra TV this morning . . ."

Riley gave Briana a puzzled look.

She made a face that said, *Well, I had to make up something!*

Riley nodded. Briana was right.

"What can I say, baby—Mr. Smith loves him some Saturday morning cartoons. Beautiful. Just show up at the country club at three. No, that's okay. They've hired a crew to set up all our gear. Beautiful. Catch you later, Gregarino. Ciao."

Briana pushed the off button on the phone.

"Score!" she reported. "Greg's wife wanted to take him carpet shopping, so three works better."

Riley checked his watch. "Okay, Granny—time for you to get into costume and makeup."

"And for *you* to put on your jacket and tie."

Riley tugged at his collar again. "Don't remind me."

At 1:30, a taxi picked up Riley, Briana, and their very large wedding gift.

At 1:44, they were waltzing down the corridors of the Brookhaven Country Club. Nobody stopped or questioned them.

Passing a wall hung with oil paintings featuring fuddy-duddy old men in suits, they saw another elderly woman. Dressed in blue. With a corsage full of blue flowers.

"Riley?" Briana whispered. "That could be the *real* Granny Smith!"

"Doesn't matter. We're in." He gestured with his empty (but beautifully wrapped) box toward the powder room door. "Now go turn into Briana Bloomfield. Quick. I'll guard the door."

"Riley?"

"Yeah?"

"You're the best!"

She gave him a quick peck on the cheek. The way a granny would.

By 2:05, sweat was dribbling down Tony Peroni's face. By 2:10 it was drizzling. By 2:12 it had dissolved most of the dye in his jet-black hair and was sending inky streaks trickling behind his ears.

Peeking through a crack in the Cranbrook Ballroom doors, Riley watched Peroni dab and blot his moist face with a big white handkerchief.

Now the bride and groom were standing in the middle of the dance floor. So were a bunch of parental-looking people in tuxedos. Several of them were gesturing at their watches. One angry man was jabbing his finger at Tony Peroni's ruffle-shirted chest.

All Tony Peroni could do was mop up more sweat and point at the empty keyboard on the stage, close to where Jake, wearing headphones, fidgeted with the knobs on a soundboard connected to Briana's portable karaoke machine.

Riley went to the powder room and rapped three sharp knuckle taps on the door.

Briana glided out in the beautiful white gown her mother had made for her and had cleaned after Jamal found it in the cafeteria Dumpster under a mountain of beanie-weenie lunch slop. She was carrying a cordless microphone that was linked to her karaoke machine.

"Do I look fabtastic?"

"Totally. Come on. Tony Peroni's dying in there."

Riley escorted Briana to the ballroom. When he swung open the doors, Jake hit a button on the karaoke machine.

The familiar *boppity-bop-bop-bop, boppity-bop-bop-bop* piano intro to "Colour My World" gave Briana time to waft angelically through the crowd and up onto the stage.

The bride and groom beamed when they recognized the opening notes of "their" song.

The parents of the bride and groom relaxed.

Tony Peroni started breathing again.

Briana launched into her number.

"As time goes o-o-on . . ."

Casey and Michele started dancing. A photographer snapped pictures.

The wedding reception was saved.

After Tony and Briana had done a couple of duets (including "Make Me Merry, Mary—Marry Me!") and Gregory Wu, the piano player, had finally shown up with a bunch of carpet samples stuffed in his sheet music case, the wedding singer gave Briana a big hug.

"Kid, you sing like a bird. The good kind, you know

what I mean? Not a crow or nothin'. You're like a song-bird when you sing."

"Thank you, Mr. Peroni. You're pretty awesome, too. It was great jamming with you."

"Can you stick around, kid? Sing a few more numbers with me and the Wu-ster?"

"Sure! That'd be fabtastic."

"What grade are you in, Briana?"

"I just finished seventh."

"So how come you didn't try out for my All-School All-Star Talent Show?"

"It's a long story . . ."

Tony held up his pinky-ringed hand. "Doesn't matter. You free next Saturday night?"

"Yes, sir."

"Good—because you, Ms. Briana Bloomfield, are my wild-card pick!"

"Whahoobi!"

A couple of hours later, Riley, Mongo, Briana, Jake, and Jamal were traipsing through the thick forest behind Mongo's house, heading to Schuyler's Pond, because it was time to celebrate.

"Dag," said Jamal. "Sara Paxton's eyes are gonna pop out of her head when she finds out you're back in the competition!"

"*And* that Mr. Peroni thinks you're the best singer

he's heard all year," added Jake.

"I can't ever thank you guys enough!" said Briana. "All of you. Really. Sincerely. I mean it, baby."

The air was thick with humidity and bugs. The towering pine trees and weedy underbrush smelled even greener in the sweltering late-afternoon heat.

"You're going to love this place, Jamal," said Briana. "There's this one rock, it's real slippery."

"We call it Slippery Rock," said Mongo.

"Like the college," added Jake.

"Yeah," said Briana, walking up the path backward so she could tell her tale with more hand gestures. "And, get this: there's this rope that's tied off to a humongous tree branch so you can swing out over the deepest part and . . ."

"Watch it!" shouted Jake.

Too late.

Briana backed into a chain-link fence.

The aluminum barrier shimmied as Briana bounced off it.

"This wasn't here last year," said Mongo. "It wasn't even here last week."

The fencing looked shiny and new. The postholes were freshly filled with concrete. A PRIVATE PROPERTY sign hung on a locked gate. Three strands of prickly barbed wire were stretched taut across the top.

Mongo sniffed the air. "This stinks."

"You can say that again," said Briana.

"No, I mean it really stinks," said Mongo.

Mongo was right: the whole forest smelled like something dead had just farted.

"IT SMELLS LIKE WHEN MY cat brings home a dead mouse," said Briana.

"Or the Dumpster behind Red Lobster during Lobsterfest," said Jake.

The rest of the gang stared at him for a second.

"Hang on," said Jamal. "This lock here is serious, folks. I should've brought my lock-picking tools."

Riley gripped the chain links. Gave one section of fence a good shake. "It's solid. Won't come down easy."

"My father has wire cutters back in the garage," said Mongo.

"We can't cut a hole in the fence, Mongo," gasped Briana. "That's vandalism. We could go to jail! And, if we did, it would go on our permanent records and none of us would ever be able to go to college except maybe that one they advertise on TV that teaches you how to drive big-rig trucks."

"Who would put up a fence in the middle of the forest?" wondered Jake.

"Probably whoever owns the property," said Briana.

"Do you think Schuyler put it up?" said Mongo. "Do you think he wants his pond back?"

"Um, Mongo?" said Jamal.

"Yeah?"

"I did a little research. Schuyler's Pond has been on the maps since 1826."

Mongo threw up both his arms. "And *now*, all of a sudden, he wants to fence it in?"

While his friends jabbered, Riley peered through the fence.

On the other side, the dirt path curved slightly and continued along the bank of the brook that fed Schuyler's Pond one hundred yards farther downstream

"Uh-oh, hold your noses," said Briana. "Wind shift."

"P.U.," said Mongo.

"Dag," said Jamal. "That is foul and malodorous."

"Yeah," said Mongo. "And it stinks, too."

"Like the Dumpster behind Bubba Gump Shrimp," said Jake. "That one's bad, too."

A sunbeam hit the rippling creek.

"Jake's right," said Riley.

"What?" said Jamal. "Somebody put a Bubba Gump Shrimp back here?"

"No. But what we're smelling is fish. Check it out."

The whole crew grabbed hold of the fence and looked where Riley was looking.

"K'nasty!" said Briana. "That is so totally disgusting."

They could see a dead, bloated fish drifting down the glistening creek on the other side of the fence.

"This is bad," mumbled Jake.

Because there were at least six more fish, all belly up, floating right behind the first one.

"We need to investigate," said Riley. "I'll climb over, take a closer look."

"Um, Riley?" said Briana.

"Yeah?"

"In case you hadn't noticed, there's barbed wire at the top of this fence."

"So it's a good thing we're here at the gate. See how this panel is about a foot shorter than the adjoining side panel?"

The others looked up to check out what Riley had already observed.

"The difference in heights makes it much easier to maneuver your legs up and over without getting scratched."

"Riley Mack," said Jamal, full of admiration, "you are

one uncommonly clever individual."

"Thanks. You guys wait here. If there's a fence to keep us out, it means somebody doesn't want us getting in."

Briana stomped her feet. "Wait. One. Minute. Why do you need to climb over there? To give the dead fish mouth-to-mouth resuscitation?"

"Well, technically, that would be a waste of time," said Jamal. "First, they're dead. Second, a fish breathes through a complex process involving water, its mouth, and its gills, whereby it extracts oxygen molecules from H_2O . . ."

"Jamal?"

"Yeah?"

"Do you ever shut up?"

"Not when I have interesting information to impart."

Briana spun around to confront Riley. "Seriously. Why are you doing this?"

"I need to gather samples."

"Of dead fish?"

"Yeah. Anybody have a plastic bag?"

"I do," said Jamal. "See, I brought a change of dry clothes, which I packed inside a Ziploc freezer bag that I will use for my swimsuit once it gets wet, which, I'm guessing, isn't going to be any time today."

"I packed a couple sandwiches," said Mongo. "And a pickle."

"Give me whatever you guys can spare."

Riley collected half a dozen empty plastic sacks and stuffed them into the side pockets of his backpack, which he tossed up and over the eight-foot barricade.

"Correct me if I'm wrong, Riley Mack," said Jamal, "but I assume you intend to run an autopsy on the dead fish to pinpoint the exact cause of this apparent ichthycide."

"This what?" said Mongo.

"Ichthycide," said Jamal. "See, an ichthyoid is any fishlike vertebrate. If someone killed a fish, they would be guilty of ichthycide. It's sort of like homicide, but with fish instead of people."

Briana groaned. "So now you're making up your own words?"

"When I have the time, Briana. When I have the time."

"You guys?" said Jake. "Why don't we just call a wildlife ranger or the EPA?"

"Ordinarily," said Riley, "a good idea. The Environmental Protection Agency would be my first choice."

"So let's let them handle this," said Briana.

Riley shook his head. "My gut tells me it's the wrong move. This fence? Whoever put it up already knows what's going on down there and they're trying to cover it up."

Riley grabbed a fistful of chain. Mongo gave him a

boost. In three swift moves, Riley was up at the corner where the gate met the taller panel.

"Swing your left leg up and over. Brace your left hand on the other side, like this. Bring your right leg up and over and—ta-dah!"

Riley clambered down to the ground on the other side of the fence.

"Let me know if anybody's coming."

"You got it," said Mongo.

Riley scampered off the path and down to the creek.

He almost gagged at what he saw.

Dozens of dead fish floating sideways on the surface of the water.

Jamal was right.

This was a serious case of ichthycide.

RILEY BAGGED A HALF-DOZEN DEAD-FISH samples and stowed them in his backpack.

He tried to make sure he had at least one of every different kind of fish he could see. A lot of them were trapped in a shallow eddy created by a cove of moss-covered rocks.

His socks were squishing inside his tennis shoes as he made his way back to the narrow path.

He wondered if whatever killed the fish could kill him. Maybe his toes were already turning black. Maybe they'd shrivel up and fall off before he hiked home. Maybe he'd mutate into some kind of alien swamp creature with gills, webbed feet, and googly fish eyes.

Maybe he watched too many monster movies.

Riley needed some grown-up assistance to get to the bottom of what had caused this fish kill. Jake was right: It was time to call in the Feds. The U.S. Environmental Protection Agency. This might be more than he and his crew could handle.

Riley changed his mind when he saw several signs staple-gunned to trees:

NO TRESPASSING
Violators Will Be Prosecuted
By Order of John Brown
Chief of Fairview Township Police

Chief Brown. Riley's old nemesis; a word Jamal had taught him. It means a rival or opponent you cannot defeat.

Chief Brown. The guy whose son, Gavin, used to be the biggest bully in town. If Brown's name was all over the NO TRESPASSING signs, that meant he was mixed up in this fish-killing mess. He had to be.

Everything Chief Brown touched usually ended up smelling worse than three-week-old bologna sandwiches stuffed in the bottom of a gym locker.

Riley's dad had once told him, "All the bad guys aren't over here in Afghanistan, son. Keep your eyes open while I'm gone. Protect your mother, defend your friends, and stand up for those who cannot stand up for themselves."

True, his dad had never mentioned brook trout or sunfish, but you can't get much more defenseless than fish swimming around in a crystal-clear stream that suddenly turns into liquid poison.

Riley reached the gate, tossed his backpack up and over.

"Careful—"

Mongo caught it.

"It's got fish gunk all over it."

"Great," said Mongo, as slimy fish juice sloshed down the front of his T-shirt. *"Now* you tell me."

"Sorry."

Riley scaled the fence and repeated his barbed-wire–clearing moves in reverse order.

"There're No Trespassing signs posted all over the place back there," he said as he climbed. "Chief Brown posted them."

"Brown?" said Jamal. "That poor excuse for a public servant? That crook, that pilferer and purloiner, that racketeer, rogue, and reprobate?"

Riley touched down on the ground. "Yeah. Him."

"Dag," was all Jamal had left to say.

"Your hunch, then, was most likely correct," said Jake. "If Chief Brown is involved with whatever's going on in the creek, bad people are undoubtedly responsible for killing the fish. The kind of bad people who could quite easily compromise a legitimate investigation."

Riley nodded. "So we forget the EPA until we know more. For now, we only work with people we trust."

"Such as?" said Briana.

Riley grabbed the backpack from Mongo. "First stop: Mister Guy's Pet Supplies on Main Street."

"Ms. Grabowski?"

"Right."

Ms. Jenny Grabowski worked at the Main Street pet store. Just out of college, she had a soft spot for animals, which Riley hoped extended to fish as well as cats and dogs.

Ms. Grabowski had helped Riley and his friends pull off what Mongo now called Operation Doggy Duty (because it made him giggle whenever he said Doggy Duty). She was also studying to become a vet tech and might have access to fish autopsy equipment, if such equipment even existed.

"Briana?" said Riley. "You're with me. We'll ask Ms. Grabowski to help us."

"Okay. But we need to cook up a good story for why we're bringing her a bunch of dead fish."

"Maybe you bought a bad aquarium!" suggested Mongo. "They sell aquariums at Mister Guy's Pet Supplies."

"Not an aquarium," said Riley with a mischievous

glint in his eye. "A pond."

"Yes!" The story started to sweep Briana away. "My mom and dad built a pond in our backyard and stocked it with all sorts of fish and shrimp and scallops."

Jake raised a finger to offer a suggestion.

"What?" said Briana, who hated interruptions when she was on a roll.

"You might want to skip the shrimp and scallops. They live in the ocean, not freshwater ponds."

"Okay. Fine. Whatever. I'm improvising here. Work with me."

Jake shrugged.

"So," said Briana, "they stocked it with all sorts of freshwater fish. Trout. Bass. Other stuff. And then, all of a sudden . . ."

Now Briana was really into it. She held her hand to her heart. Tears welled up at the corners of her eyes.

"I went out back to play fetch with Binky, my favorite fish."

Jake raised another finger.

"Okay, fine," said Briana. "Rewrite: I went out back to bask in the beauty of Binky, my silvery, shimmery fishy friend and . . . and . . . she was dead, Ms. Grabowski! Dead!"

Here Briana fell to her knees and wept a bunch.

"That'll work," said Riley, with a nonchalant nod.

"That was beautiful," said Mongo.

"You were amazing," added Jake.

"Personally," offered Jamal, "I think you overdid it a little with the weeping."

"Fine. I'll make an adjustment. I'm an actress. I can take notes. Let's go, Riley. We're on!"

"OH MY," SAID MS. GRABOWSKI. "That's horrible, Briana."

"Yes," sobbed Briana. "As you might imagine, I am devastated."

"How are your parents holding up?"

"Hmmm?"

"Your parents. You said this was their fishpond."

"Oh. Right. They're totally bummed, too." She gripped her hands together in the classic beggar gesture. "We need to know what killed our fishes, Ms. Grabowski! Can you help us? Please?"

"Of course, Briana. And it's fish."

"Whaa?"

"The plural of fish is *fish*."

"I know. But I'm overwrought with emotion and, when I'm overwrought, my grammar suffers."

"Have Pepe and Amigo been in your backyard?"

"My Chihuahuas?"

Ms. Grabowski nodded. "If they drank any of the pond water, they might need to be taken to the vet. Immediately."

"Fortunately," said Riley, "Briana's dogs are not allowed in the backyard."

"My parents are afraid they'd scare the fish."

"So, *whew!*" said Riley. "We don't have to worry about the dogs. Just the fish."

"Well," said Ms. Grabowski, "we haven't really gotten into aquatic autopsies at vet tech school. Not yet anyway."

"Do they have a lab?" asked Riley.

"Several. But . . ." She pried open the plastic Baggies on the checkout counter.

Rotting fish funk filled the air.

The stench was overwhelmingly awful because the carcasses had been sealed up inside hot plastic.

"I don't dink you beed a lab, Riley." Riley figured Ms. Grabowski was trying to say she didn't think they needed a lab. But she was holding her nose.

"How com-buh?" Riley was holding his nose, too.

"Dis meddy bifferet fish." She quickly resealed the bags. "This many different fish, we know what killed them: water pollution."

"You're positive?" asked Riley.

"Yes. If only one species of fish had died, then it would be possible that the cause of death was some kind of virus endemic to that species."

"Endemic?"

Where was Jamal when you needed him? thought Riley.

"Sorry," said Ms. Grabowski. "College word. *Endemic* means 'exclusively confined to one species.'"

"Like they caught flounder flu?" suggested Briana.

"Or something else. Maybe a strain of bacteria that only attacks trout. But since there are several *different* species in your sample, then you're most likely looking at lack of oxygen in the water caused by pollution." She turned to Briana. "Do your parents use lawn fertilizer in the backyard? Do they pour on lots of chemicals to kill weeds?"

"No," said Briana. "They're totally organic. Anti-chemicals, antifertilizer. They probably use composted banana peels."

"Well, do you live downhill from a factory or a gas station or any kind of toxic chemical dump?"

"I sincerely doubt it. We live in a very ecologically friendly environment."

"They have their own windmill," added Riley.

"And solar panels," said Briana.

"Well, something bad got into your pond water. You need to get a sample and have it tested for contaminants."

The next morning, Riley, Jamal, and Mongo returned to the rutted dirt road behind Mongo's house and, once again, followed it up into the forest.

"This time, I packed my lock-picking tools," said Jamal.

"Excellent," said Riley.

"Hey, Riley?" said Mongo.

"Yeah?"

"What're we gonna do with the water once we scoop it out of the creek?"

"Take it to Ms. Kaminski."

"The science teacher?"

"Yep. She's totally into all sorts of forensic stuff. She watches every one of those CSI shows on TV and has set up her science lab to be like a mini–crime lab."

"So," said Jamal, "she could check out our water. Put it under the microscope and tell us what kind of toxic chemicals are floating around inside it."

"Exactly. And if she can't, she'll know who can."

They reached the chain-link fence.

There was a new, fluorescent orange sign attached to it:

No Trespassing
By Order of
Fairview Police Department

"Uh-oh," said Mongo. "They could arrest us for tres-passing if we go any farther."

"Nah," said Riley. "They'll arrest us for breaking and entering first. Jamal?"

Jamal grabbed the padlock and inserted a slender metal tool up into its keyhole. The sleek pick looked a little like that thing a dentist uses to poke your teeth to see if you have cavities.

"Cake," said Jamal when the lock's hasp popped open.

"Okay," said Riley. "I plucked most of the dead fish out of a pool just beyond those bushes."

"Should I relock the gate?" asked Jamal. "In case somebody else comes along while we're down by the stream?"

"No need," said Riley. "This will only take like a sec-ond." Riley pulled a twenty-four-ounce sports bottle out of his backpack and twisted open the lid.

The three friends hurried up the path, through the

woods, and down to the muddy creek bank.

"This is horrible," said Jamal.

"Yeah," said Riley as he crouched to scoop up the water sample.

Jamal and Mongo were staring at the water in disbelief. Dozens and dozens of dead fish floated in the shallow pond where water pooled behind a row of rocks before rippling its way downstream. There were so many white-bellied fish littering the surface of the creek that it looked like someone had dumped tons of upside-down hamburger buns into the stream.

"We got to figure out what's killing these fish," said Mongo. "It could probably kill us, too."

Jamal just nodded. He was struck dumb by the sight of all the poisoned fish.

"That should do it," said Riley, tightly resealing the cap on his water bottle. "I sent Ms. Kaminski an email last night. Told her, even though school was officially out, me and Mongo were working on a science project. She was impressed. Said she'd meet us in the lab at eleven."

Jamal glanced at his watch. It was ten. "We better hustle."

"Yeah. Come on."

Riley, Mongo, and Jamal clambered up the creek bank.

As they neared the gate, they heard voices.

"Quick!" said Riley. "Hide!"

They ducked into the bushes.

"You see?" said a very familiar voice. "I had my men post a few more signs. Should keep out any looky-loos till your people clean things up."

It was the police chief!

"WE DON'T NEED TO CLEAN it up, John," grumbled the second man. "We own it."

Riley recognized the second voice, too: Sara's father, Mr. Paxton, the country club president.

"Well, Prescott," said the chief, "don't forget who foreclosed on this land for you in the first place. Made it possible for you to snatch up the whole forest, dirt cheap."

"*Nyes*, Chief. I just wish you had moved a little faster."

"Sorry," said the chief, not sounding sorry at all. "I got busy."

"Right," said Mr. Paxton. "That thing with your mother and the dogs."

"We were framed. Set up."

"I'm certain you were. My goodness, something smells fetid."

"Huh?"

"Something stinks."

"Hey," said Brown, "don't look at me. I took a bath last night. It's the fish. All that rain Sunday must've stirred things up."

"We should hire a crew to cart away the carcasses," said Mr. Paxton. "Before someone complains about the odor!"

"Don't worry. My son's all over it. He and a few of his high school buddies will swing by and eliminate all the evidence."

"You hired high school students?"

"Yeah."

"But—"

"Don't worry, Prescott. I handpicked the kids. These boys won't squeal about this to anybody. They wouldn't dare. I have outstanding warrants on all of them."

"They're criminals?"

"I prefer the term *juvenile delinquents*."

Riley crawled a few inches forward. Through a break in the brush, he could clearly see Mr. Paxton and Chief Brown.

"So," said the chief, "what about Kleinman?"

"What about him?" said Paxton.

"People might've reported this stench to *him*. There's a whole tract of houses just beyond that treeline."

"I'll take care of Kleinman," said Mr. Paxton. "He's swinging by the club at four. I've invited him to be a celebrity judge at the talent show this coming Saturday."

"Celebrity? Kleinman? He's bald."

"Look, John—you take care of the little fish, I'll deal with the bigger ones."

The two men quit talking.

Riley heard someone jiggle the lock.

"John," said Mr. Paxton, "why is this gate unlocked?"

Riley's heart leaped up into his throat.

"Gavin," muttered Chief Brown. "He hung the extra signs for me last night. Forgot to lock up. That boy fell out of the stupid tree and hit every branch on the way down."

The chief snapped the lock shut.

"What if somebody else went in *after* Gavin?" asked Mr. Paxton. "What if it was Kleinman or some of his people?"

"Then I would've heard something by now. Relax, Prescott. You're fine. Now let's get out of here. I hate the woods. Too many bugs."

The two men walked out of view. Car doors opened and closed. An engine roared to life. Wheels rumbled down the dirt road.

Riley, Mongo, and Jamal remained frozen until they heard the car accelerate onto the paved roadway a quarter mile away.

"Can we breathe yet?" Mongo finally whispered.

"Yeah," said Riley. "They're gone."

"Brown *and* Paxton?" said Jamal. "They're both mixed up in this thing?"

"So it seems," said Riley, standing up and brushing dirt off his jeans.

"Might I say, Riley Mack, that you were wise not to report this matter to the proper authorities because, if you ask me, the authorities around here aren't all that proper."

Riley nodded. His mind was racing a mile a minute. What could Brown and Paxton be working on together? And who was this Kleinman guy they both seemed to be so worried about? Why did they need to bribe *him* into silence?

"I need to be at the country club at four p.m. to check out this Kleinman character."

"I'll come with you," said Jamal. "Do they let black people into this country club?"

Riley shook his head.

"They don't? What is this, 1952 or something?"

"No, I mean I don't want you coming along. You're too young. This is too risky."

"Risky? Risky is my middle name."

105

"Really?" said Mongo. "Mine is Horatio."

"Hubert Horatio Montgomery?"

Mongo nodded.

"Man, what is wrong with your parents?"

Before Mongo could answer, Riley interrupted. "I'll go with Briana."

"What?" said Jamal.

"We snuck into the wedding reception without a problem. She can wear the same disguise and we'll sneak in again. Nobody ever bothers old people or asks them for ID. We can whip up a second costume for me."

Jamal looked skeptical. "You're gonna be another old lady?"

"No. I'll still be her grandson." Riley was smiling. He loved it when a plan started coming together in his head.

"And what are you two going to do for wheels?" asked Jamal. "We can't afford another taxi and you can't make your granny ride her bike to the country club."

"Hey!" said Mongo. "My dad has a golf cart in the garage. Somebody traded it in when they bought a used car."

"Really?" said Jamal. "And your dad took it?"

"Sure. He'll take anything. Golf carts. Motor scooters. Chickens."

"Did it come with golf clubs?" asked Riley.

"Yep."

"Okay. We'll call Briana. Have her put on her granny outfit and whip me up a blond wig, polo shirt, and blue blazer; maybe give me a pair of horn-rimmed glasses. I want to look like I belong at Brookhaven."

"All right," said Jamal, "it might work."

"Pop open that gate again, Jamal. Mongo and I need to head back to school."

"School," said Mongo sorrowfully. "Some summer vacation this turned out to be!"

PRESCOTT PAXTON DID NOT LIKE working with Chief
Brown.

But he needed the idiotic buffoon's assistance
because this thing was much, much bigger than making sure the grand reopening of the Brookhaven golf
course went off without a hitch.

"So," asked Chief Brown as Paxton piloted his Mercedes down shade-dappled Brookhaven Lane, "your
daughter's performing at the talent show this Saturday?"

"Nyes," said Paxton.

"This general that's going to be one of the judges,"
said the chief, "is he the reason you're doing the whole

Greens for the Army Green theme?"

"Of course not, John. The Brookhaven Country Club is an extremely patriotic institution. It's why we also asked Mrs. Madiera Mack to help judge the talent competition."

"Bad idea, Prescott. Big mistake."

"How so? Her husband, Colonel Richard Mack, is a decorated war hero."

"I don't care. Her son is a KTM—a known trouble-maker."

"Really?"

"Riley Mack is the one who framed my mother. Shut down her farm."

"Is that so?"

"I can't prove it. Not yet. But I will. You'll see."

They passed through the imposing gates of the country club. As they cruised up the driveway, Paxton admired the emerald-green grass of the golf course's rolling fairways.

"What kind of fertilizer you guys use?" asked Chief Brown. "Miracle-Gro?"

"I'm not certain. You'll have to ask our head grounds-keeper, Stuart Sowicky. He has been coordinating the lawn-grooming efforts with the landscaping company."

"Yeah, right," said Chief Brown sarcastically. "I'll be sure to do that."

Paxton pulled the Mercedes to a stop under the club's

canopied entryway. Two college-age parking attendants in scarlet vests dashed over to open the doors.

"Good morning, Mr. Paxton!"

"Welcome back, Mr. Paxton!"

"Boys." Paxton handed over his key fob.

"Where's my car?" asked the chief, hiking up his pants.

"We'll bring it right up, Chief Brown."

"You do that, son. And don't you even think about hitting the siren."

"No, sir. I mean, yes, sir."

Paxton said his good-byes and headed off toward the east wing of the country club. As club president, he had a small but tastefully furnished room with a desk and a telephone to use for official club business.

Walking up the impressive, hardwood-paneled hallways, Paxton passed a photo exhibit titled *Brookhaven: A New Golf Course for the New Millennium*.

The pictures showed the progression of work on the massive landscaping project: President Paxton in a hard hat plunging a golden shovel into the dirt to break ground; backhoes digging trenches in the earth at night under the hazy glare of spotlights; bulldozers, flecked with snow, smoothing out rich, black soil; landscapers laying down sod in the early spring; a dump truck emptying sand into liver-shaped pits; pipe valves being opened to fill a water hazard.

In one photo, Stuart Sowicky, the head grounds-keeper, could be seen consulting with a landscaping architect over an unrolled set of landscaping plans. The two of them were pointing at something remarkable on the horizon, as if they were both Balboa, discovering the Pacific Ocean.

"I dig that picture, too."

Paxton turned around. It was Sowicky himself, his mustache droopy, his chin and cheeks unshaven for days. Sowicky kept his long silver hair tied back into a ponytail. Paxton sniffed the air and smelled an odor very similar to dog poop. He also noticed that Sowicky's green jumpsuit was muddy at the knees; his tan work boots were caked with what could have been clay (or something worse).

"Stuart," Paxton said smugly.

"Dude," said Sowicky, who called everyone *dude*. "So—you have a chance to check out those *other* pictures? The ones I gave you?"

"No. As you might imagine, I've been rather busy."

"Sure. I can dig it. But . . ."

Paxton held up his hand. "I will look at your photographs as soon as we're through with the grand reopening. I promise."

"Okay. That's cool."

"*Nyes*. Nice bumping into you, Stuart."

"Likewise. Later, dude." Sowicky loped up the hall toward an exit.

Paxton realized: he lived his life surrounded by idiots.

Which, in a way, was a good thing.

It made it much, much easier for *him* to be a diabolical genius.

AT ELEVEN A.M., RIGHT ON schedule, Riley and Mongo met Ms. Kaminski in the parking lot of Fairview Middle School.

She had two bumper stickers plastered on her tiny car: CSI: CAN'T STAND IDIOTS and SUPPORT YOUR LOCAL POLICE—LEAVE FINGERPRINTS.

"Looks like we're the only ones here," said Ms. Kaminski. "Even the janitor has started his summer vacation."

"How can you tell?" asked Riley.

"By reading the evidence."

"You mean like footprints and junk?" said Mongo.

"No. His parking space. It's empty. Come on. Let's

head inside to the science lab."

They entered the school.

"We really appreciate you helping us out like this," said Riley as Ms. Kaminski flipped on the lights to the lab.

"Hey, you guys could be goofing off at the pool. Instead, you're here doing science. I'm impressed!"

"Okay," said Riley, showing Ms. Kaminski the screen to his smartphone. "These are the fish we found dead in Mongo's mom's pond."

"Interesting," said Ms. Kaminski, studying the first picture. "Rainbow trout."

Riley thumbed a button on his phone. "Here's a bluegill, a bass, a perch, a . . ."

"Mr. Montgomery—just how big is your parents' pond?"

"It's, you know, a regulation-size pond," said Riley, since it had been his idea to place the pond in *Mongo's* backyard this time instead of Briana's because Mongo's house was closer to where they had found the dead fish.

"Well, it certainly is well stocked."

"Here's the water sample," said Riley, pulling the sport bottle out of his backpack.

"My boyfriend, Ron, has agreed to check it for toxins," Ms. Kaminksi said. "He works at a lab that does all sorts of bacteriological and chemical testing for people using private well water. Things are slow this week, so he'll do it for free."

"Awesome," said Riley.

"Easy for you to say. I owe him dinner and movie."

"We can help with that."

"Riley gets free passes to everything," added Mongo.

"Really?" Ms. Kaminski was impressed.

Riley shrugged. "What can I say? I have many friends in many places."

"I'll tell Ron to look for fertilizers, pesticides, herbicides, household chemicals—stuff like laundry detergent and cleaners."

"What about gasoline and oil?" suggested Riley.

"Sure. Is the pond downhill from your garage?"

"Um, I think so," said Mongo.

"Then gas, oil, and antifreeze definitely go on the list. See, we need to figure out the watershed's possible pollution sources."

"Watershed?" said Mongo.

"The area of land that drains to a creek, lake, aquifer, or, in this case, backyard fishpond. Do you have a topographical map of the area around your house, Mongo?"

"We can get one," said Riley.

"Do. Because water flows . . ."

Mongo jumped in: "Downhill!"

"That's right."

"So," said Riley, "while your friend figures out what's in the water, we'll figure out what's uphill from the pond and try to ID all the possible sources of contamination."

"Exactly!"

Riley and Mongo met the other guys downstairs at Jake's house.

"How's Briana doing on the costumes for this afternoon?" Riley asked.

"She biked over to the thrift shop to pick out the rest of your preppy wardrobe," said Jake. "Khaki shorts, argyle socks, polo shirt, ascot."

"Ascot?"

"A silk scarf you wear around your neck, like Richie Rich in the comic books," said Jamal. "You're gonna look sharp, Riley Mack. Sharp!"

"Cool."

"Not completely," said Jake.

"What do you mean?"

"While Briana was biking over to the store, Sara Paxton zoomed by in somebody's convertible and started screaming junk at her."

Riley sighed. "Such as?"

"Loser, cheater, ugmo."

"To state the obvious," said Jamal, "that blond

balloon-head is furious Briana made it into the talent show finals."

Mongo gasped. "Sara may try to hurt Briana!"

"Don't worry," said Riley, even though he, himself, was worried about the same thing. "We won't let her."

"Okay," said Mongo. "Good."

"Did you guys find a topographical map?"

"Over here," said Jake. "Computer three."

Riley checked out the screen. It was filled with swirling brown lines, splotches of green, and blue squiggles.

"These contour lines represent changes in elevation. I've zoomed in on Schuyler's Pond. The closer the contour lines, the steeper the incline. The green, of course, represents forest. The blue lines are creeks and streams."

"And the brown," said Jamal, "is dirt. Because dirt is, you know, brown."

Riley tapped a blue line. "This is where I found the fish. What's uphill from that spot?"

"Follow me to computer two."

Jake rolled his desk chair sideways to a different monitor.

"We synched up Google Earth with the topo map. This is satellite imagery of the same area."

"Hey!" said Mongo. "There's my house. I recognize our swing set."

"As you recall," said Jake, "when we hiked into the woods, we had to go *up* a hill to get to the dirt road."

"So," said Riley, "the pollution, whatever it is, isn't coming from any of these downhill houses."

"Exactly," said Jake. "Our contaminant has to come from the north."

"What's up that way?" asked Riley. "A farm? Some kind of factory?"

Jake tapped the zoom toggle to widen out the image.

Riley saw trees bordering several oddly shaped areas of green that were occasionally interrupted by small pools of water or kidney-shaped sand pits.

"The golf course?"

"Exactly," said Jake.

"So that explains the new fence, the No Trespassing signs, and why Mr. Paxton was tromping around in the woods with Chief Brown. He's president of the country club."

"Dag," said Jamal, "these Paxton people are vile, despicable, *and* atrocious. While Sara's trying to steal Briana's scholarship, her daddy's busy bumping off fish!"

"REMEMBER," SAID RILEY, TWISTING THE steering wheel on the battery-powered golf cart, "our primary objective is to find out who this Kleinman guy is."

"I know why we're going to the country club, you young whippersnapper," cackled Briana, totally into character as a wrinkled old grandmother. She was wearing a purple tracksuit, like retired people do (the better to stuff her butt and legs with foam padding). A golf visor circled her bubble of blueish-white hair and shadowed the jeweled cat's-eye glasses perched on her bumpy nose.

The electric vehicle whirred and clicked as it scooted up the cart path toward the main entrance to the club.

Riley was in costume, too, including a "preppy boy" blond wig that hid his most distinguishing physical trait: his fiery red hair.

"Do I look like I belong?" he asked Briana.

"Totally," she said, dropping her crotchety voice. "So, how do we find this Kleinman guy?"

"We look for Mr. Paxton. He'll probably be coming out front to meet Kleinman at four."

"What time is it now?"

Riley glanced at his watch. "Three fifty-eight."

"Step on it, Sonny!" said Briana.

Riley jammed down the accelerator and zipped up the curvy asphalt strip.

The fact that Mongo's house was just on the other side of the ridge from the golf course meant that it took Riley and Briana only about fifteen minutes to drive the four miles in their quiet little cart.

"There're a bunch of carts lined up over there," said Briana.

Riley piloted the vehicle under the veranda, passing two valet-parking attendants.

"Welcome back, Mrs. Smith!" one of the college-age guys called to Briana as they zipped past.

Briana gave him a Queen of England window-washer wave. "Hel-lo-o-o-o, dear!"

"That's the guy who helped you out of the cab Saturday," whispered Riley.

"Check," Briana whispered back.

Riley slid their cart in between two others.

"Need a hand with your clubs, Mrs. Smith?"

Great. The car jockey wanted to help them unload their cart.

"That's okay," said Briana. "My grandson Richie is here to help me today."

Riley gave the guy a jolly finger wave.

"You storing those in the clubhouse?" the guy pulled a pad and pencil out of his back pocket. "I'm like you, Mrs. Smith. Can't wait for the course to reopen on Saturday."

"You bet your sweet bippy," chirped Briana. "I'm eager to hit the links and shoot a birdie!"

The guy tore the top sheet off his pad and strode closer to the cart. "Let me grab those bags for ya, Richie."

"Richie?" Briana tweedled to Riley. "Where are my teeth, dear? I was soaking my dentures in your soda-pop cup. The scrubby bubbles clean 'em up good. . . ."

Riley walked over and took the slip of paper from the grossed-out parking attendant. "Don't worry. I help her with her chompers . . . and the clubs."

The guy gave Riley a grateful thumbs-up and hustled back to his post.

Riley walked back to the cart. "Well played, Briana."

"Thanks. This makeup works best at a distance. So

what do we do till Paxton shows up? I can't just stand here gumming my lips."

"We could mess with the golf clubs, I guess."

"Yes! Props!"

Riley and Briana slipped around to the rear of the cart and started futzing with the knitted club-head covers.

"Richie, you put the *P* on the nine!" Briana knuckle-punched Riley in the arm.

"Sorry, Grandma."

They fiddled with the heads of all the clubs, switching the covers back and forth, then forth and back.

"Here he comes," said Riley.

Mr. Paxton marched out through the front doors of the country club.

"Can we get you your car, Mr. Paxton?" asked one of the valet-parking guys.

"No, thank you. I'm meeting someone."

"Where's Kleinman?" muttered Briana, who had started reorganizing the golf balls stuffed into the zippered pouch on the side of the bag.

"Hang on," said Riley as a car appeared down at the front gate and crawled up the long driveway.

Riley squinted. It was a pretty nondescript automobile. White. Standard grille and bumpers. Probably a Ford.

"Ah," said Mr. Paxton. "Here he comes."

"Who is it?" Briana whispered to Riley.

"Can't tell. Not yet."

Finally a small, bald man in glasses climbed out of the plain white car. He looked like a timid mouse with a driver's license.

"Hello, Irving," said Mr. Paxton.

"Prescott." The two men shook hands. Well, Mr. Paxton pumped while Mr. Kleinman more or less flopped along with every jerk of his arm. "I must say, I was rather surprised to receive your invitation. . . ."

"You're free Saturday night, I trust?"

"Oh, yes. Of course. I have no conflicts. No plans. Seldom do on a Saturday night . . ."

"Excellent!"

"But, well, truth be told, I've never judged a talent contest before."

"Have you ever seen *American Idol*?"

"Once. I was visiting my mother and she had it on."

"Then you know how it's done. Let's step inside, shall we? We can discuss the details of your duties with Carol Goans and Kristen Lamoreaux."

Mr. Kleinman fidgeted with his glasses. "Who are they?"

"Two of the young women on the program committee. Both recently divorced, which gives them more time to volunteer. They're inside and can't wait to meet you."

123

"Really?" Mr. Kleinman laughed like an asthmatic donkey.

Paxton snapped his fingers. "Boys? Take care of Mr. Kleinman's car."

"Yes, sir, Mr. Paxton. Right away, sir."

Both parking attendants trotted over to take the shy guy's keys.

Kleinman handed off his keys with another wheezy donkey laugh. "Enjoy the ride, fellows. But remember—it's a government vehicle. If you exceed the posted speed limit, it's considered a federal offense."

First clue, thought Riley. *Mr. Kleinman works for the federal government.*

The second clue came two seconds later.

AS MR. PAXTON ESCORTED MR. Kleinman toward the country club doors, the parking guy goosed the little white car and whipped it into a sharp left turn.

Riley and Briana could both clearly see the decal plastered on the passenger-side door: a stylized green flower, with two leaves, its round head filled with wavy blue water, flat green earth, and baby-blue sky.

The flower graphic was encircled by these words: UNITED STATES ENVIRONMENTAL PROTECTION AGENCY.

"He's with the EPA," gasped Briana. She was so shocked, she dropped the golf balls she'd been pretending to sort. They ping-ponged and hopscotched across the asphalt.

One ball bounded to the left and bonked Mr. Paxton in his butt.

He turned around to pick it up.

Riley dropped his eyes. He didn't want to be recognized.

"Is this your ball, ma'am?" Mr. Paxton called from across the parking lot.

Now Riley heard footsteps.

"Irving," Riley heard Mr. Paxton say, "why don't you wait inside with the ladies?"

"Okay," said Kleinman, snorting out another donkey laugh.

The footsteps drew closer.

In fact, they scuffed to a stop right behind the golf cart.

Riley, his head still bowed, could see the shiny tips of Mr. Paxton's shoes.

"Here you are, ma'am."

Out of the corner of his eye, Riley saw Mr. Paxton plop the dimpled white ball into the palm of Briana's hand.

"You know, Briana, the next time you play dress-up, you should remember to apply wrinkles to your hands as well as your face. And, if you're going to give yourself a grandson, I suspect you can do better than Riley Mack, who, I recently learned, is a well-known trouble-maker around town."

Briana's hand started to tremble.

Riley's did not.

He looked up, smiled his goofiest grin, and said, "Aren't these amazing costumes, Mr. Paxton? What are Sara and the Starlettes wearing?"

"I beg your pardon?"

"This is Briana's costume for the talent show Saturday night!"

Briana mouthed a silent "Wha-huh?"

Mr. Paxton arched a skeptical eyebrow. "You're in the finals, Briana? Sara informed me that you missed the audition at school."

"But then Tony Peroni heard her sing," said Riley, "and—BOOM! She's his wild-card pick. Isn't that awesome?"

"Nyes," said Mr. Paxton.

"She's thinking about doing that old Beatles song. You know: 'When I'm Sixty-Four.'"

"I am?" whispered Briana.

"Sure. It'll be totally *hilarious* when you sing it dressed up as an old lady dancing with her walker. So, what are Sara and her group doing for the show?"

"Something a bit more patriotic," Mr. Paxton answered coldly. "In keeping with the evening's theme."

"Cool!" said Riley. "I'm sure my mom and the general will *love* that!"

"*Nyes*. Does your mother know you're running around town, stirring up more trouble?"

"Trouble? She's the one who asked us to swing by and see what kind of dress you think she should buy for Saturday night when that Pentagon general's in town. You still want the general to meet the local war hero's wife, right?"

Mr. Paxton blinked. Several times.

"Nothing formal. Whatever she is comfortable wearing I'm certain will be fine."

"And how about me? Is this a good look for me?"

"You look preposterous."

"Is that a good thing?"

"No. Lose the ascot *and* the wig."

"Gotcha. Less 'Richie Rich,' more 'Peter Preppy.' Thanks!"

Mr. Paxton turned to Briana. "Congratulations on earning the wild-card slot. However, you should know: We have hired Sara and her chums a choreographer. A *Broadway* choreographer."

"Really?" said Riley. "Are they going to be the witches from *Wicked*?"

"No, Mr. Mack. They are going to *win*. Therefore, Miss Bloomfield, I suggest you withdraw from the competition and spare yourself any *further* embarrassment. Good day, children."

Mr. Paxton tromped triumphantly back into the country club.

"Man," said Riley when he was gone, "I am so glad we did not contact the EPA. That Kleinman guy is probably on Paxton's payroll, too."

"*Nyes*," said Briana, mimicking Mr. Paxton perfectly. "I suggest you withdraw from the ichthycide investigation, Mr. Mack, and spare yourself any further embarrassment."

"Wow," said Riley. "You nailed him!"

It was Briana's turn to shrug. "No biggie. He's such a pompous windbag, his voice is extra easy to imitate."

Wheels started spinning in Riley's head. "Could you do it again?"

"*Nyes*, dear. But of course."

"Excellent. We might need it."

"For what?"

"For what we're gonna do next!"

"What's that?"

"I don't know yet."

"Well, I might be busy."

"Huh?"

"Riley, you just told the president of the country club that I'm singing a Beatles song in old-age makeup on Saturday night."

"I think it would be cool."

"Riley? I don't know any Beatles songs!"

"Okay, skip the Beatles. You could be . . . Fairview's very own Rapping Granny!"

"You mean that old lady who was on *America's Got Talent*?"

"Yep. It's granny time!"

"Fabtastic!" said Briana. "Granny is in the house!"

Then she popped mouth noises the whole cart ride back to Mongo's.

RILEY HAD AN IDEA OF what he should do next but he wanted to run it by his father first.

Since bumping into Mr. Paxton and Mr. Kleinman, he had cooked up a scheme to get *adults* to contact the EPA about the water pollution.

Lots of adults.

It was almost 10 p.m. in Fairview, which meant it was almost 6:30 a.m. *tomorrow* in Afghanistan. Riley had his laptop fired up and would video-link with his father at 22 hundred hours on the dot, which was military talk for 10:00 p.m.

Outside, it was pouring. Rain pattered on the roof and slashed against the windowpanes. This much rain meant there would be a ton of water racing downhill from the golf course toward Schuyler's Pond.

And that meant there would, most likely, be a ton more dead fish floating in the creek tomorrow morning.

Riley's mom stuck her head in his bedroom door.

"You getting ready to call your dad?"

"Yeah."

"Say hi for me, hon."

"You want to talk to him first?"

"Nope. I get him all to myself at twenty-three hundred hours."

Riley gave his mom a two-finger salute. "Roger that, Mom."

She saluted right back. "Over and out. Have fun."

She pulled his door shut. His mom and dad both thought it was very important that Riley be able to talk to his father in private on a regular basis. "Just in case there's any guy stuff you two need to talk about," his mom always said.

Riley waited until the glowing red digits in his bedside alarm clock flipped from 9:59 to 10:00.

He pushed the return key, placing the call.

The videoconferencing software did its thing. A grainy window opened, the boxy pixels coming together to create the digital image of a soldier in chocolate-chip camo.

"Hey, Da—"

Riley did not finish that thought.

The soldier on the screen wasn't his father.

"Um, I think I have a wrong number or something," said Riley.

"Negative," said the soldier. "Riley, I'm Sergeant Kenny Lorincz. I have the distinct honor of serving in Colonel Mack's Ranger battalion. Unfortunately, your father will be unable to chat with you today."

"Is he okay?"

"Roger that. However, several of our troops are not."

Riley winced a little when the soldier said that. "Did they get hurt in a firefight or something?"

"No, sir. We are currently bivouacked on base. Getting three hot meals a day. Taking showers."

"Oh. Well, that sounds good. . . ."

"Agreed. It *sounds* excellent. However, the chow being served in the dining hall isn't agreeing with some of our men."

"Too spicy or something?"

"Your father suspects some of the food is tainted. We have several men who need to be evacuated out for non-combat-related illnesses. Nausea, vomiting, fever, chills. Couple guys have developed kidney stones. Extremely painful situation."

"What happened?" asked Riley. "Did the enemy sneak into the mess hall and put poison in all your food or something?"

"Too early to speculate, Riley. However, your father is determined to uncover the truth, no matter who tries to stop him. He will not rest until this issue is resolved."

Riley grinned. *Like father, like son.*

"Is there anything I might be able to help you with tonight?" asked the sergeant. "Do you have homework? I'm quite good with algebra. Very bad with spelling and punctuation."

"School's out for the summer."

"Outstanding."

"There is one thing."

"Yes?"

"You ever hear of a General Joseph C. Clarke?" Riley had hoped to ask his father that question.

"Hang on," said Sergeant Lorincz. He swiveled away from the laptop at his end to tap on a keyboard attached to a second computer. "I'm checking our personnel database via a secure satellite uplink," he said over his shoulder. "Here we go." The sergeant swiveled back to face Riley. "Can I ask why you need to know this information, Mr. Mack?"

"It's for a, um, a project."

"I thought you said school was out for the summer."

"Yeah. It is. This is more like a personal project. For my mom. She has to meet this General Clarke at a 'salute the troops'–type dinner at Brookhaven

Country Club this weekend."

"And you want to help her out, let her know how she can make table talk with the general?"

"Yeah. Something like that."

"I see now why your father is always bragging about you."

"He is?"

"Twenty-four/seven."

Riley blushed. Just a little.

"Tell your mother that General Joseph C. Clarke serves out of the Pentagon as chief procurement officer for the United States Army's Near East military operations."

"What's that mean?" asked Riley.

"He's an extremely important pencil pusher. Buys all the stuff we need out here in the field. Blankets, uniforms, tents, food. Everything. If you want to do business with Uncle Sam, you need to do business with General Joseph C. Clarke first."

"Oh. Okay. Cool. Thanks, Sergeant Lorincz."

"My pleasure. One more thing, Riley."

"Yes, sir?"

"I have the unwelcome duty of informing you that your father will be unable to link up with you or your mother for a period of several days; not until, as he put it, he 'gets to the bottom of this mess hall mess.'"

"I understand. You guys have enough to worry about

over there. You shouldn't have to worry about your food trying to kill you, too!"

"Roger that. Will you pass on word to your mother as to our situation?"

"Yes, sir."

"Appreciate it."

Riley saluted the computer screen as the soldier's image faded out of view.

"Poor Dad," he mumbled.

It sounded like the food over in Afghanistan was even worse than the slop in the school cafeteria.

EARLY THE NEXT MORNING, RILEY and his crew gathered once again in Jake Lowenstein's basement.

The heavy rains had stopped around two or three in the morning. Now the sun was out and shining bright.

"I've cooked up a little scheme I call Operation Water Hazard," Riley said to his assembled troops.

"Lay it on us," said Jamal.

Riley untied the string clasp on an interoffice envelope his mom had brought home from her job at the bank and dumped out its contents on a worktable.

"I wrote down everybody's assignments on index cards." He handed one to Briana. "Work on your imitation of Mr. Paxton. Jake?"

"Yeah?"

"I need you and Jamal to help Bree out." He handed them both cards. "Search the internet. See if you can find voice recordings of Mr. Paxton."

"Should be easy," said Jamal. "Big blowhard like that? He's probably out there all the time, pontificating profusely. Ya'all know what *pontificating* means?"

"Yes," said Briana. "'To speak in a pompous manner.' Just like you."

"I am not pompous, Briana. I am precise."

"You guys?" said Riley. "Fish are dying out there. Our swimming hole is totally polluted. Work with me."

"Sorry," said Briana.

"I also express remorse for my pedantic proclivities," said Jamal.

"Huh?" said Mongo.

"He means he's sorry," said Briana.

"I found some intel on Mr. Paxton," said Jake.

"Already?" said Riley. "Excellent! What can you tell us?"

"He's not only president of the Brookhaven Country Club, he's chairman and chief executive officer of Xylodyne Dynamics."

"Xylodyne is humassive!" said Briana.

"Yes," said Jake. "They have operations in more than seventy countries, hundreds of subsidiaries, affiliates, branches, divisions. . . ."

"They're like their own country," said Mongo.

"Probably have their own army," said Briana. "My parents are always going to anti-Xylodyne rallies and protests."

"And," said Jake, "Xylodyne does about a bajillion dollars in business with the Pentagon."

"Well," said Riley, "that explains why Mr. Paxton is trying to brownnose General Joseph C. Clarke: he's the guy who signs the bajillion-dollar checks."

"But why's he kissing the EPA's butt?" asked Jamal.

"Probably because he knows his golf course renovations are responsible for what's happening down in that creek. Mongo?"

"Yeah?"

"You're with me." He handed Mongo a card.

Jamal raised his hand. "Um, Riley?"

"Yeah?"

"What's with the note cards, man?"

"I dunno. Mr. Phelps always had an envelope with junk stuffed in it on *Mission Impossible*."

"He did!" gushed Briana. "This is so cool. We're like our own TV-show-slash-major-motion-picture franchise. Some day, an actress will play me: an actress playing people who *aren't* me!"

"But my card is blank," said Mongo.

"Yeah," said Riley. "Sorry. My hand kind of cramped up on me after a few cards. Anyway, you're with me.

We're heading back to the creek to see if we can ID the source of this pollution."

"Okay," said Mongo. "I'll write *creek* on my card in case we get split up or something."

"Good idea. Jake?"

"Yes, Mr. Phelps? What is my mission, should I choose to accept it?"

"Lock onto the GPS chip in my cell phone."

"No problem."

"Track us."

"Still no problem."

"Overlay our position on that topographical map of the creek and country club; let us know if we leave the watershed contours. Jamal?"

"Yo?"

"I need to borrow your lock-picking tools."

Luckily, Jamal had been an excellent instructor.

Riley inserted a stainless-steel file from his younger friend's leather kit into the padlock, flicked it a couple times, and popped open the hasp.

"We're in," he whispered to Mongo, who had grabbed Jake's aluminum baseball bat "just in case we run into somebody besides dead fish."

Riley pushed open the gate. He and Mongo stepped into the no trespassing zone. Then Riley closed the gate and slipped the lock back through the fencing so he could reattach it on the other side.

"Um, Riley?" said Mongo. "Why are you locking us in?"

"We many not be the only ones checking out the creek this morning."

Mongo hefted up his baseball bat.

"Come on." Riley led the way through the brambles to the creek bank. Once again, they were staring down at dozens of floating fish carcasses.

"This way," said Riley, splashing into the shallow water. "It's only about six inches deep. We'll walk the creek upstream."

Mongo waded in after him.

There were clumps of dead fish ringing both their legs. The creek water had a scummy fish-oil slick oozing across its surface.

"This is so gross," said Mongo

"Just don't look down."

"I can feel dead fish bumping into me. They're cold and slimy—like floating slabs of snot."

"Okay, okay," said Riley, slogging toward the far shoreline. "We'll take the land route."

"Thank you!" said Mongo.

They hauled themselves out of the stream. Riley touched his Bluetooth earpiece and said, "Call Jamal."

The voice-activated dialing system engaged with a dial tone followed by string of bleeps and bloops.

"That you, Riley Mack?"

"Yeah. You and Jake got us on the map?"

"Ten-four, Eleanor. You should head upstream maybe twenty feet. When you come to where it bends a little, hike up the hill through the trees. That'll take you to the golf course."

Riley heard a clicking noise in his ear. "Hang on, Jamal. I have another call."

Riley was about to tap his earpiece again when Mongo raised his bat.

"Somebody's comin'!" he whispered.

"Take cover!" Riley whispered back.

"What's going on?" asked Jamal.

"We have guests." Riley and Mongo ducked behind a patch of berry bushes.

The second call clicked in Riley's ear again.

He'd have to let it roll over to voice mail.

"Riley?" said Jamal. "What's going on, man? Who's out there with you two?"

Riley answered as quietly as he could.

"Gavin Brown."

23

RILEY WAS CROUCHING IN THE bushes, eyeballing Gavin Brown and his buddies through a hole in the thorny branches.

"I could take them all out," said Mongo, dragging his bat closer.

"Shhh," said Riley, because he wanted to hear what Gavin and his goons were grousing about.

"Ten dollars an hour isn't enough to pick up dead fish," he heard one of the high school guys moan.

"Well, if we don't do what he tells us to, my father will arrest us all for those other things he knows we did."

Riley, of course, recognized Gavin. His flat flounder

face was one of a kind. Well, among humans. The dead creatures floating in the creek all had Gavin's beady eyes, smooshed-in nose, and puckered lips. Gavin, who used to terrorize all the younger kids at Fairview Middle School until Riley intervened, was a big ox. His friends were even bigger and oxier. There were six of them, sloshing through the creek.

"It's too hot to work," complained one of the thugs.

"The sun makes the fish smell even worse," added another.

"Do we have to do this now?" whined a third. "*Mortal Death Kombat Three* opens today."

"No way," said the main complainer.

"Totally," replied the movie buff. "Plus, if you go to the very first show, you get a free Mortal Death Kombat drinking cup and squiggle straw!"

"This sucks! I have been waiting, like, all year to catch that flick!"

"Well, when's the first screening?" asked Gavin.

"In an hour, man," said the movie maniac.

"Then let's go!" said Gavin.

"Really?"

"Hey, my dad just said we had to come back again on account of the rain last night. He didn't say *when* we had to come back!"

"How about tomorrow?"

"Sounds good to me!"

The six goons whooped, high-fived, and hightailed it back to the dirt road and took off.

"Okay," said Riley. "They're gone for the day. Jamal? You still there?"

"Yeah."

"I need to check my voice mail. The caller ID shows it was Ms. Kaminski beeping in. Meanwhile, you guys should hit everybody's garages and backyard storage sheds. Round up as many ice chests as you can."

"Are we putting together a picnic?"

"No. A bucket brigade. I'll be back after I check my messages."

Riley thumbed a few digits on his smartphone. Punched in his voice mail ID.

"Hello, Riley, this is Ms. Kaminski. As we suspected, there are seriously elevated amounts of nitrogen in the water sample you took from Mrs. Montgomery's fishpond. I'd look for any heavy lawn fertilizing, either in their yard or the neighbors'.

"Ron also said he found other trace elements, including large quantities of cyanuric acid, which is sometimes used in bleaches, disinfectants, and herbicides. So, again, I think we're looking for somebody using lots of lawn-care chemicals. Hope this helps. Oh, and thanks for the gift certificate you dropped off at school this morning. I've never eaten at the Quilted Dove but everybody says it's the best restaurant in town."

Riley shrugged. The Dove was okay. If you were a grown-up and liked stuff like striped bass tartare and couscous instead of pizza and fries.

"Anyway, good luck tracking down the source of your pollution! So long."

Riley disconnected the call.

"Come on," Riley said to Mongo. "We need to head upstream and uphill."

They followed the creek until they reached the bend Jamal had mentioned. Using trees for handholds, they hauled themselves up a very steep hill. They were approaching the edge of the forest when Riley's earpiece buzzed again.

"This is Riley. Talk to me."

"Hey, it's Jake."

"Where's Jamal?"

"With Briana. Looking for ice chests."

"What's up?"

"I'm tracking you on the topo map. You should be approaching the fairway behind the country club."

Riley and Mongo stepped out of the trees into the high grass fringing the golf course, what golfers called "the rough." The woods they had hiked through were littered with tiny white balls.

"There should be a knoll of some kind to your left," said Jake.

"Yeah. The fairway slopes up to a little pond . . ."

"A water hazard," said Jake.

"Exactly. And above that, there's a plateau with a flag planted in it. It's the putting green for the ninth hole."

"Okay," said Jake, "that plateau corresponds to the drainage divide. Surface runoff from everything downhill of it flows through the forest to the creek and then down to Schuyler's Pond."

"Hang on," said Riley. "Somebody's coming again." He motioned for Mongo to slip back into the darkness under the trees.

"Who is it?" asked Jake.

"It sounds like heavy equipment," Riley reported. "Probably part of the landscaping crew."

"No," said Mongo, from his vantage point behind a pine. "It's a farmer."

A man dressed in bright green coveralls was circling the ninth hole green on a small lawn tractor. Behind the canopied seat and big rear tires Riley saw what looked like a fertilizer spreader; a mechanical spinner for slinging out chemicals—probably pellets of nitrogen-rich fertilizer and pesticides to make the golf course's new grass look so unbelievably lush and green.

"We've got our guy," said Riley. "Tell everybody to put on their swim shoes. We need to head back to the

147

creek tonight and pick up a few fish."

"How come?" asked Mongo.

"Operation Water Hazard is about to become Operation Stink Bomb."

THAT NIGHT, AROUND 9:30, RILEY, Mongo, Jamal, and Jake hiked up the dark dirt road to the locked gate.

Briana wasn't with the fish-gathering crew. She was totally panicking about the Saturday night talent finals and needed to rehearse her rapping-granny act.

"Whoo," said Jamal when he caught his first whiff of dead fish. "I believe we have just discovered the *real* reason Briana could not join us tonight: I suspect Eau de Fishsticks is not her favorite brand of perfume."

"All right, you guys," said Riley, as he swung the beam of his flashlight back and forth across the black surface of the water. Bloated white bellies were everywhere. Dead fish were floating downstream like Styrofoam burger boxes on a rafting trip. "Scoop up as many fish as you can. Load them into the ice chests."

Each member of the crew carried a cooler and his own version of a fishnet; Jake trawled with a tennis racket, Jamal skimmed the water with his mother's spaghetti strainer, Riley used a lacrosse stick, and Mongo trapped dead fish in the webbing of his first-baseman's glove.

They hauled cold, clammy carcasses—many without eyeballs anymore—out of the stream and dumped them into their carriers, where they landed with wet, sloppy slaps.

"This is beyond gross," said Jamal.

"Try breeding true your mout," said Jake, breathing through his mouth.

"I did," said Mongo. "But I sucked down too many mosquitoes."

"Come on you guys," said Riley, sloshing through the scummy water. "Just a few more."

"Ry-wee?" said Jake, still holding his nose.

"Yeah?"

"What exact-wee are we going too doo wiff all dese dead fish?"

"Put them where grown-ups will smell 'em and start asking questions."

"In their mailboxes?" said Mongo.

"No," said Riley. "We need adults to confront that

golf course gardener for us; the guy puttering around on his tractor, pumping out poison to make the greens look so freakishly *green*."

"So, what do we do next, Riley Mack?" asked Jamal. "Because I've got about ten pounds of pure stinkitude packed in my dad's cooler here. He's never, ever going to want to have a backyard barbecue again. The dang fish ooze is soaking straight into the plastic walls. That stench isn't ever coming out! What's the plan, man?"

"Simple," said Riley, squeaking the lid back onto his cooler. "We're going to give these fish a proper funeral in a much more public body of water. Jake? Is the wind still supposed to come out of the south tomorrow?"

"Hang on." Jake quickly glanced down at his glowing smartphone. "Correct. No change on my WeatherBug app."

"Then we go with the water hazard below the ninth hole. The wind will blow across it and send the stench straight up to the country club. When people sit down to breakfast on that outdoor sundeck tomorrow morning, they'll be directly upwind of a newly polluted pond."

Riley and Mongo led the way up through the woods to the fringes of the golf course.

"Douse your lights," whispered Riley.

The guys all turned off their flashlights.

"Follow me."

Riley trotted out of the rough, onto the fairway, fishy water sloshing in his ice chest the whole way. Some sludge splashed out when the lid flipped up an inch, permanently odorizing his faded black T-shirt. The whole crew was dressed in black tonight. Black jeans. Black T-shirts. Black sneakers. Mongo had even put some of that black gunk football players use under his eyes, which made him look like an enormous raccoon sporting a buzz cut.

"Hunker down," said Riley, as they headed up the hill toward the water hazard. "Keep low and keep quiet."

The gang crept across the shag carpet of clipped grass as quietly as cats wearing fuzzy bunny slippers.

Lights were on over in the country club. Riley could hear laughter. Tinkling music.

"Is there a dance or something tonight?" whispered Jake, moving stealthily at Riley's side.

"I don't think so. Probably just people eating dinner inside at the restaurant."

"Hope they're enjoying their seafood salads," said Jamal. "Because, I'm sorry Long John Silver's, I may never eat fish again."

The foursome reached the lip of a shallow pond.

"Okay. Slip your fish into the water," said Riley. "Easy. Try not to make too much noise. It's better if they don't discover this mess till morning."

"How come?" asked Jamal.

"When the sun's up, it'll be way easier for us to see the grossed-out looks on all their faces!"

EARLY THE NEXT MORNING, AFTER their parents had all left home for work, Riley's crew piled into Mongo's golf cart and scooted over to the country club.

They entered the asphalt golf cart path via a nontraditional route: Riley drove the electric buggy straight through a four-foot-wide gap in the country club's hedgerow boundary that he and Mongo had scouted out the previous day on their bikes.

"There's the ninth hole," said Jamal, pointing at a triangular flag flapping in the distance.

"Wind's still blowing the way we want it to," added Jake, using the fluttering pennant for a windsock. "Out of the south, heading north."

"Excellent," said Riley. "Time for a little off-roading. Hang on everybody."

He swerved sharply, leaving the narrow paved path for the grass.

"Ri-i-i-ley?" stuttered Briana as the cart bounded over roots, ruts, and rocks. "P-p-p-please! I ha-a-a-ad a bi-i-i-ig bre-e-eak-fast!"

"Not m-m-me," said Jamal. "I had t-t-toast. D-d-dry t-t-toast."

Riley swung the cart behind a thick stand of trees and eased on the brake.

They were just south of the water hazard, hidden in the shadows of the forest.

"All right," said Jamal, who had brought along a pair of binoculars, "we already have some interesting action up on the outdoor dining deck."

"What do you see?" asked Riley.

"Under the second yellow umbrella. Four ladies fanning the air under their noses and examining their plates. Looks like they all went with bagels and lox this morning. I believe they are currently contemplating the freshness of their smoked salmon."

"Excellent," said Riley.

"They're calling for their waiter. Okay. Here he comes. He's sniffing their food. Now he's sniffing the air all around him. Looks like he just smelled a skunk fart."

"Even better," said Riley, linking his hands behind his head and propping his feet up on the dashboard of the golf cart to savor the moment.

"The elderly couple two umbrellas to the right are sniffing their cereal bowls," reported Jake, who had brought along his collapsible telescope. "They're calling for the waiter, too."

"You guys?" said Mongo. "Here come some golfers."

"Ah," said Riley. "Our first foursome of the day."

"I thought the course wasn't open till Saturday," said Briana.

"Not officially," said Riley. "But maybe these guys just couldn't wait."

"Maybe they're chums of mine," said Briana, slipping into her Paxton impersonation.

"Another distinct possibility," said Riley with a laugh.

"Facial expressions indicate the gentlemen have picked up the stench," reported Jake.

"Big time," added Jamal. "Duffer in the pink plaid pants looks like he wants to hurl. Of course, I would, too, if I ever wore pants that looked like that."

"This is fabtastic!" said Briana. "Way to go, Riley!"

"Thanks," said Riley, sighing contentedly. "I love it when a plan works even better than we planned. Briana?"

"Yeah?"

"Please stand by."

"Will do." And then she started warming up. "A Tudor who tooted a flute tried to tutor two tooters to toot."

"Okay," said Jake, "the gentlemen on the ninth hole are pointing down at the water hazard."

"They have seen the fish," said Jamal. "Repeat, they have seen the fish!"

"Awesome," said Mongo. "This is gonna work, Riley!"

He shrugged casually. "I figured it might."

"One of the guys is waving his golf club over his head," reported Jake, "trying to get that waiter's attention."

"Another gentleman is using his cell phone to call somebody," added Jamal. "My guess? The country club or the cops. Maybe both."

"Well, then," said Riley, "I guess we should make a phone call, too? Briana: you're on!"

"*Nyes*, Riley. But of course."

Briana switched on the pitch modulator, then pressed the speed dial for Mr. Kleinman's office at the Environmental Protection Agency.

"Irving?" said Briana when Mr. Kleinman answered. "*Nyes*, Prescott Paxton here. Hate to bother you, old chap, but something *fishy* is going on over at my country club."

Briana broke out the ice-cold juice boxes. Riley tore open a tube of Oreos and passed it around. Jake popped open a bag of popcorn and shared it with Jamal.

Secluded in the shadows of the trees, Riley and his crew had front-row seats for the most entertaining golf-course comedy since *Caddyshack*.

Within an hour, a crowd of twenty, maybe thirty agitated adults stood around the water hazard, pointing at the dead fish, holding their noses, making stinky-cheese faces, looking for someone to blame.

Sheriff Brown showed up and barked a bunch of orders into a squawking walkie-talkie.

Next to arrive, maybe ten minutes later, was Mr. Kleinman from the EPA. He was toting an aluminum briefcase, which he snapped open to extract some glass tubes and rubber gloves.

Finally, Mr. Paxton arrived.

"This. Is. So. Awesome!" said Briana.

"We saw a wrong and righted it," said Riley.

"It's what we do, man," said Jamal proudly. "It is what we do."

Now Mr. Paxton was on his cell phone yelling at someone.

Five minutes later, a lawn tractor came chugging over the rise.

"And we have a winner," said Jake as the man in the green coveralls climbed off his riding mower.

"Busted!" said Mongo.

"Um, Riley?" said Briana.

"Just a sec. I want to hear this." He leaned forward and picked up snatches of Mr. Paxton's tirade.

"This is your fault. . . . What kind of head grounds-keeper . . . ? How much fertilizer . . . ? Pesticides . . . this is inexcusable . . ."

"Riley?" Briana whispered tensely.

"What?"

"We got the wrong guy!"

"Huh?"

"I know that man in the green coveralls. It's Mr. Sowicky!"

"And?"

"He's the guy who taught my parents all about organic gardening. He's an eco-freak. No way did he kill those fish with chemicals."

THIS IS ABSOLUTELY, UNBELIEVABLY PERFECT, thought Prescott Paxton as he stood atop the ninth hole.

He motioned to Chief Brown.

"You want me to arrest Mr. Green Jeans?" the burly police officer asked eagerly. "Slap the hippy-dippy groundskeeper in handcuffs?"

"No. Not yet. Tell me, was it your son Gavin's idea to haul the fish out of the creek and fling them into this water hazard?"

The chief rubbed his cheeks and thought about his answer.

"Well, uh, maybe . . . I'll have to ask."

"If it was, kindly inform Gavin that he and his friends

have earned my respect as well as a hefty bonus."

Chief Brown beamed when he heard Paxton use the word *bonus*.

"Well, Prescott, to tell you the truth, I more or less gave Gavin the idea."

"I see. And was it also your idea to call Mr. Kleinman from the Environmental Protection Agency?"

The chief narrowed his eyes and rubbed his cheeks some more. "You happy to see Kleinman taking water samples?"

"Delighted."

"Well, I figured you might be," said Chief Brown, hiking up his baggy khakis. "So I gave Kleinman a call. Told him something was, you know, fishy up here."

"*Nyes*. Excuse me. I must have a word with my head groundskeeper."

"I've got the cuffs standing by."

"Splendid. Mr. Sowicky?"

Pretending to be furious, Paxton stomped down the lush green slope from the hole to the water hazard where the ponytailed tree hugger stood shaking his head and staring down at all the foul-smelling dead fish.

"Mr. Sowicky? What goes on here?"

"I don't know, man."

"I do," said Kleinman. He was shaking some sort of stoppered test tube. "I ran a quick field test. Your nitrogen levels in this water are off the chart!"

"What did you do, Stuart?" Paxton demanded indignantly.

"I-I-I . . ."

"I'll tell you what he did," said Kleinman. "He used all sorts of toxic fertilizers and pesticides on this grass to make it artificially green!"

"No, man," said the groundskeeper.

"If you did this thinking you could impress me and the board by greening up the fairways in time for opening day, you were sorely mistaken."

"No, I swear . . ."

"I suppose I'm partially to blame," said Paxton with a sad shake of his head. "Giving you free rein. Allowing you to handle the groundskeeping chores as you saw fit. Not providing adequate supervision."

"Mr. Paxton, I—"

Paxton shot up his hand. "Not another word. Frankly, Stuart, I have heard enough of your lies. Yes, you have given us a lush and beautiful lawn, but at what cost?"

He gestured sadly toward the dead fish floating belly-up in the little pond.

"Mr. Sowicky?"

"Yes, sir?"

"You are fired!"

"B-b-but—"

"Mr. Kleinman?"

"Yes, Prescott?"

"You might want to send a team downhill from here. It will probably prove prudent to investigate the entirety of this watershed area. I dread to think what might have happened farther downhill in that ravine."

"The creek!" gasped the EPA geek. "Schuyler's Pond!"

"*Nyes*. Fortunately, Xylodyne Dynamics recently purchased all that acreage. I don't think my company will sue *my* country club. However, we should clean up the environment. If not for ourselves, for the children."

He turned to the crowd of onlookers.

"Remember, ladies and gentlemen: None of us really own the land. We merely borrow it from our descendants."

Every head was nodding except the silly groundskeeper's; he looked stunned.

Too bad.

The police chief shot out his hand toward Sowicky. "Give me the keys to the tractor, beatnik. We can't have you driving that thing around town, spreading poison all over the place."

"B-b-but—"

"You want to add some jail time to your EPA fines?"

"No, I—"

"Then give me the keys, take a hike, and get the heck off of this golf course! Your boss just fired you."

With his head hanging low, his hands jammed into the sagging pockets of his coveralls, the heartbroken groundskeeper shuffled across the fairway toward his maintenance shed.

Poor, poor man, Mr. Paxton thought as a small, almost imperceptible, grin slid across his lips.

Stuart Sowicky would shoulder all the blame for this ecological disaster. In front of at least two dozen witnesses, the slow-witted sluggard had been tried, convicted, and sentenced.

The EPA would clean things up and, if toxic chemicals should happen to leach out of the soil to spoil the water for years to come, well, everybody would know exactly whom to blame: the overeager groundskeeper.

Meanwhile, Mr. Paxton's earth-shattering, company-crushing secret would remain safe.

No one would ever uncover the truth!

RILEY COULDN'T REMEMBER A TIME when he had felt worse.

This made back-to-back busts for his "brilliant" schemes. First, he'd cost Briana the middle school talent show crown by being wrong about the roller skates. Now, he'd made the wrong man lose his job. All of a sudden, his Gnat Pack's troublemaking was causing too much trouble—especially for the people they'd been trying to help.

"Briana, do you know Mr. Sowicky?"

"Sort of. He's come by the house a couple times. Once he brought my parents worms for their compost heap."

"Okay. You're with me." He turned to the guys. "You three head back to Jake's basement. We need to regroup."

Mongo raised his hand to ask a question.

"Yes?" said Riley.

"Don't we also need a new plan? Because, I'm sorry, this last one, it was fun and all, but it didn't turn out so good."

"I know, Mongo."

"So we're gonna fix it, right?"

"We better," said Jamal. "This is our second lame operation in a row. One more strike, and we're out."

Riley sighed. He couldn't disagree.

"Look, guys, I need to go apologize to Mr. Sowicky. Then we'll figure out what we do next. Come on, Bree. Do you know where he keeps his stuff?"

"He has like a trailer. It's just through those trees on the other side."

Briana and Riley hiked across the fairway while the rest of Riley's dejected crew headed back to Jake's house.

"I feel terrible," Riley mumbled. "We framed an innocent man!"

"So, we'll *un*frame him," said Briana.

"How?"

"I don't know, but I'm not worried. You're like an idea hamster, Riley; your wheels are always spinning.

166

You'll think of something fantabulous."

Riley nodded grimly.

He *would* think of a way to save Mr. Sowicky. If not? Well, he'd just have to avoid reflective surfaces for the rest of his life, because he'd never be able to look at himself in a mirror again.

"There it is," said Briana.

They had come into a clearing behind a stand of trees, where they saw two white trailers sitting catty-corner to each other. Both had wooden steps leading up to an attached porch.

Riley quickly surveyed the scene. The ground here wasn't as manicured as the rest of the golf course. In fact, the only landscaping around this backstage area was hardpan clay, scraggly weeds, and patches of gravel.

Riley saw a couple of compost bins made out of recycled root beer barrels and several sacks of something called "Zoo Poopy Doo." He also noticed a backhoe—with a toothed bucket on a boom at one end, a bulldozer plow at the other—and a rolling generator-floodlights combo parked between the two mobile homes.

"Which trailer is Mr. Sowicky's?" Riley asked Briana.

She did a rapid fire eeny-meeny-miny-moe between the two. On the final *-moe* her finger ended up pointing to the left.

"That one!" she declared.

Riley bounded up the short staircase. He was all set to bang on the thin metal door when he heard loud voices on the other side.

"Just tell Mr. Paxton to cool his freaking jets," said the first voice.

"We finished that particular job last week," said the second.

"Yo," said the first voice, "not for nothin', but Curly here reminds me that we finished that particular job last week."

"So why's Paxton still bustin' our chops about it?" said the second voice, the guy named Curly. "Ax him that, Larry."

"Yo: Why's Paxton still bustin' our chops about this freaking landfill project over here?"

Both men, Curly and Larry, had what Riley would describe as a street-smart edge to their voices.

"They sound like mobsters!" Briana whispered in his ear.

Okay. That, too. With their thick accents, the two men inside the trailer sounded like the hoodlums who worked for Da Boss in every cheesy gangster movie ever made.

"Ah, fuhgedaboudit!" the man named Larry shouted. "Go tell that nimminy-pimminy Paxton to take a flying leap off a galloping goose. Right. Have a nice day."

Riley heard a telephone slammed down so hard, the bell in its base jingled.

"Wrong trailer," he whispered to Briana.

"Definitely."

The two of them very quietly tiptoed down the wooden steps. They were on the final tread when they heard the flimsy trailer door swing open behind them.

"Yo?" said the voice Riley recognized as belonging to Larry. "Youse two lost or somethin'?"

Riley and Briana whirled around.

Two men (with bodies much smaller than their thuggish voices had suggested) stood on the makeshift porch. Both were dressed in blue construction-worker coveralls and bright yellow Bob the Builder hard hats.

The younger one was maybe four foot four in his work boots.

The older guy looked like a short grumpy pear. His neck was tiny. His stomach wasn't.

"Yo?" said the grumpy one. "You heard Larry. Youse two lost?"

Okay. The grumpy, dumpy one had to be Curly. The younger, dumber one was Larry.

"Yes, sir, I'm afraid we have lost our way!" said Briana, putting on her best "Mary Had a Little Lamb" innocence act.

"We're looking for our uncle," said Riley. "Mr. Sowicky."

"He's the golf course's head groundskeeper!" said Briana.

Curly jabbed a thumb toward the other trailer.

"He's next door."

"Thank you, ever so much," said Briana, dipping into a curtsey.

"Whatever," said Curly as he and Larry clomped down the steps.

"'Scuse us," said Larry. "We got work to do."

"Yeah," added Curly. "Golf course is supposed to open this Saturday. We better go finish the freaking eighteenth hole."

As the two construction workers walked away, Riley read the embroidered patches stitched on the backs of their jumpsuits: ACE CONSTRUCTION—A SUBSIDIARY OF XYLODYNE DYNAMICS.

Xylodyne.

The men who'd just been complaining about Mr. Paxton *worked* for Mr. Paxton.

Interesting, thought Riley.

And what was all that talk about a "landfill"?

Suddenly, Riley was extremely glad they'd knocked on the wrong door first!

"AND SO, SIR, I JUST wanted you to know how sorry I am," Riley said to the ponytailed groundskeeper, who was taking framed photographs off the walls of his trailer and placing them inside a cardboard box.

"You're Riley Mack?"

"Yes, sir."

"*The* Riley Mack?"

"Um, I guess."

"Cool," said Mr. Sowicky as he stuck out his hand to shake Riley's. "Always wanted to meet the little dude who helped out Cheyenne."

"Who?" said Riley.

"Cheyenne Woody? Fairview Middle School? A group

of girls was picking on her, calling her names. You organized everybody on the playground. Got them to turn the name-calling into a funny song-and-dance routine?"

Briana knuckle-punched Riley in the arm. "Remember that one? It was like an episode of *Glee* out there on the monkey bars! Even the mean girls joined in on the chorus. One of your best ever, Riley! Definitely in the top ten."

"Legendary stuff, little dude," said Mr. Sowicky. "Legendary."

"Well, they were picking on Cheyenne something fierce."

"I know, man. Cheyenne is my niece."

"No! Way!" said Briana.

"Way," said Mr. Sowicky who looked to be fifty-some years old even though he sounded like he was maybe eighteen. And a surfer. "My sister, Cheyenne's mom, told me the poor kid would come home from school sobbing every day until some illustrious dude named Riley Mack did her a skillfully executed solid. Never forgot the name, man."

"So," said Briana, "you're not mad at us?"

"Of course not. Anger is one letter short of danger."

"But, we cost you your job," said Riley.

"I was going to quit anyway. Something fishy's going

on around here—and I don't mean the dead trout you dudes tossed into that water hazard." Mr. Sowicky took another photograph off the wall. "See that dude there?"

"Yeah," said Riley, studying the picture of a young man who might've been Mr. Sowicky thirty years before, shaking hands with a bald guy in a business suit.

"That's me, man. Back in the day. And the bald dude? That's Mr. Jordan Bowling, my first club president. In the past three decades, I've had maybe fifteen different bosses, all of them exceptionally cool. They were the ones who encouraged me to do my job in an eco-friendly fashion, long before it became trendy. The last president, the one before Paxton, he's the dude who told me about the Zoo Poopy Doo."

"I saw the bags out front," said Riley. "What is it?"

"Elephant manure from the Louisville Zoo, man. Makes excellent organic fertilizer."

"So you never used, like, bad chemicals?" said Briana.

"Never."

"See?" said Briana. "I knew he wasn't the bad guy!"

"So, Mr. Sowicky," said Riley, "do you have any idea what's killing the fish down in the creek?"

"Okay, here's the deal, little dudes. This is like Watergate, only worse."

"Huh?" said Riley and Briana together.

"A cover-up and a conspiracy."

"What's going on?" asked Riley.

"It's Paxton, man. That devious and diabolical dude is up to something shady."

"Like what?"

"Well, for starters, he had his cronies from Ace Construction tear up all my fairways and greens. Had them bulldoze mountains of dirt all last fall and into the winter and now it's what?"

"The middle of June," said Riley.

"Exactly," said Mr. Sowicky with a slightly crazed look in his eyes. "That's what I'm saying, man."

"Um," said Briana, "they're just, you know, renovating the golf course."

"Then why'd they put it back together wrong?"

"Huh?" said Riley.

"Dude, I have an elevation app in my iPhone!"

"And?"

"The greens, the tee boxes, the rough—everything is like three feet higher than it used to be!"

"Well," said Briana, "they probably added fresh top soil or something."

"Three feet deep?" Mr. Sowicky's eyes were wide and wild.

"So, uh, what do you think is going on?" asked Riley.

"I took pictures, man!"

"Of what?"

"The bulldozers and backhoes. Working all through the night. Digging huge honking trenches in the ground, plowing crap in."

"What kind of crap?"

"I was too far away to see exactly what they were dumping in the ditches but it couldn't have been good or they would have done it in broad daylight, right, man?"

"Did you use a digital camera?"

"Yeah."

"And did you shoot high-resolution images?"

"Totally."

"Then," said Riley, "just blow up the pictures on your computer and you'll see what they were burying."

"Awesome idea," said Mr. Sowicky. "Only one problem. I gave the camera to Mr. Paxton before I downloaded anything."

"What? Why?"

"Because I foolishly put my faith in the integrity of the office of the country club presidency, man."

"And what did Mr. Paxton do with your digital camera?"

"He locked it inside his top desk drawer. Said he'd look into the matter right away. But I saw him the other day and he said he'd been too busy worrying about the grand reopening to even take a peek at my pix. Probably erased them all."

"Why would he do that?" asked Briana.

"Because, here's the part I failed to realize before I gave the fox the keys to the henhouse: Xylodyne Dynamics, of which Mr. Paxton is like the head honcho, is a multinational, multifaceted corporation."

"And?" said Riley.

"Dude, Xylodyne has its greedy fingers in everything: defense contracting, agriculture, food services, oil, plastics, chemicals, and . . ." Mr. Sowicky looked around the room to make sure there weren't any spies lurking in the corners. "Waste management, man!"

"What?" said Briana. "You think they used the Brookhaven golf course as a garbage dump?"

"Totally."

It was crazy, but it might make sense. It would also explain why Curly and Larry had mentioned a "landfill" project.

"So," said Riley, "you think Mr. Paxton had the landscaping guys from Ace Construction, a Xylodyne company, rip up this golf course and turn it into a dumping ground for, I don't know, toxic chemicals from one of their plastic plants or something?"

Mr. Sowicky nodded. "That's what's killing the fish, little dudes. It's why Paxton pushed for the total golf course makeover the minute he became club president. Xylodyne Dynamics needed a top-secret landfill, a place where they could dump some of their seriously evil garbage!"

"IN SHORT," SAID RILEY, "SINCE we can't dig up the golf course, we need Curly and Larry to dig it up for us."

"Who?" said Mongo.

"These two teeny-tiny construction workers we met," said Briana.

"They're not tiny," said Riley.

"Um, the tubby one is like four feet tall. And the other one, the one who never learned to breathe through his nose, he might be pushing four and a half, but only because his work boots have heels that are like three inches tall."

Riley could not dispute Briana's observations.

The two of them had just returned from the country

club to join up with Jake, Mongo, and Jamal down in Jake's basement.

"You really think they buried something bad under the golf course?" said Mongo.

"Bad?" said Briana. "Try torrific!"

"Torrific?" said Jamal. "I'm afraid I am not familiar with that expression, Briana."

"It means terrible *and* horrific. Look it up."

"Oh, I will," said Jamal. "I will."

"You guys?" said Riley. "I need your undivided attention. The new plan I've worked out is extremely complex. If just *one* piece is out of place, the whole house of cards comes tumbling down."

"What's it called?" asked Mongo eagerly.

"Huh?"

"What's the name of the new plan?"

Okay. That was the one thing Riley hadn't thought about.

"Um, Operation Whack-A-Mole."

"Really?" said Jamal. "Does this new plan involve rodents with uncanny burrowing ability?"

"No. Just a lot of holes."

"We could call it Operation Swiss Cheese," suggested Mongo. "That has lots of holes, too!"

"Fine. Operation Swiss Cheese."

"How about Operation Mulligan?" said Jamal. "See, in golf, a Mulligan is a do-over; a shot that isn't counted against your score. And since our first shot, Operation Stink Bomb, was so lousy, I believe we are in serious need of a Mulligan."

"Fine," said Riley. "The new plan is called Operation Mulligan. Now, then—"

"Stew," said Mongo. "I like mulligan stew."

"I liked *Mike Mulligan and His Steam Shovel* when I was little," said Jake.

"The book?" gushed Briana. "Me! Too! Remember when the steam shovel had to become the furnace because it forgot to build a ramp when it dug—"

"Guys?" said Riley. "Seriously. We need to pull together on this caper or, I guarantee, it will not work. Worse, Mr. Sowicky will stay fired while Mr. Paxton and his Xylodyne pals keep on polluting that creek and our swimming hole."

Nobody said anything for a very long thirty seconds.

"So," said Briana, finally, "how does Operation Mulligan work?"

"Yeah," said Jake. "I'm in, whatever it is."

"Me, too," said Mongo.

"I've been in," pouted Jamal. "It's why I came up with the name in the first place."

"Okay," said Riley, "first things first. We need to make sure Mr. Paxton won't be snooping around the golf course tomorrow. Jake?"

"Yeah?"

"Can you find his phone number?"

"Home or office?"

"Office. Xylodyne Dynamics. We know Mr. Paxton is still at the country club, dealing with the fallout from Operation Stink Bomb."

Jake clacked his keyboard. "Got it. His direct line. And his executive assistant is Ms. Ginger J. Bowes."

"Briana?"

"Nyes?" She was already in character.

"Let's find out what Mr. Paxton has on his calendar tomorrow."

Jake handed Briana a headset patched into the pitch filter and then passed around wireless earbuds so the rest of the gang could eavesdrop on the call.

The phone made two soft, purring rings and was snatched up.

"Mr. Paxton's office, this is Ms. Bowes speaking. How may I direct your call?"

"Ginger?"

"Good afternoon, Mr. Paxton. How are things at the country club?"

"Fine. Dandy."

"Were you able to take care of that . . . issue?"

"Nyes. The lad from the EPA lent a hand. We fired the head groundskeeper."

"Good for you, sir."

"*Nyes.* Firing people is what I do best. Remember that, Ginger."

"Yes, sir. Of course, sir."

"So, tell me: What does my calendar look like tomorrow?"

"The same as it looked this morning when we went over it."

"And you expect me to remember what we discussed this morning? I'm a busy man, Ginger. I need an executive assistant who can answer my questions when I need them answered or *re*answered!"

"Yes, sir. Of course, sir. You will be with General Joseph C. Clarke, from the Pentagon, all day tomorrow."

"Um-hmm."

"You two are touring the food processing plant from nine a.m. to noon."

"*Nyes.*"

"Returning here for lunch in the executive dining room."

"And after lunch?"

"You're in the board room with General Clarke and the team from marketing."

"Hmmm. Busy day."

"Yes, sir."

"Guess the general and I won't be able to sneak away

for a quick eighteen holes at the club, eh?"

"Not until Saturday, sir. You and the general will be in the first foursome to hit the links when the course officially reopens at eleven a.m."

"Excellent. Thank you, Ginger. Keep up the good work."

"Thank you, sir. And, if I may . . ."

"Nyes?"

"Have you been able to consider that cost of living adjustment we discussed?"

"You mean your raise, Ginger?"

"Yes, sir," the secretary said meekly.

"Very well, put yourself down for twenty percent. No. Wait a minute. Make that thirty percent."

"Thank you sir!"

"Can you do my signature?"

"Of course, sir."

"Then kindly put through the papers. Affix my signature. Buy yourself a new hat."

"Yes, sir. I will, sir."

"And, Ginger?"

"Sir?"

"A word to the wise: If later today I should happen to ask you, once again, about my schedule, please do not remind me that we have already discussed it *twice*."

"Of course not, sir."

"Good. And, that raise?"

"Sir?"

"Let's make it easy on the boys down in accounting: just double whatever you're making now."

"Yes, sir. Thank you, sir."

Riley made the cut sign. Jake disconnected the call.

Then the whole crew applauded, whistled, and hooted as Briana took a well-deserved bow.

"OKAY," SAID RILEY, PACING AROUND the basement, "we know that Mr. Paxton won't be anywhere near the country club again until Saturday morning."

"That's good," said Mongo. "Right?"

"It's better than good. It's perfect. Jake?"

"Yeah?"

"Does your dad still have that Underground Surveyor Apparatus he brought to the beach last summer to look for buried treasure?"

"It's in the garage."

"Did he find any treasure?" asked Mongo.

"Some bottle caps, a couple quarters, and a high school class ring from 1983."

"Awesome!"

"Remind me of the USA's capabilities," said Riley.

"It's the best country on earth!" said Mongo.

"I'm with Mongo," said Jamal, leaning back in his swivel chair. "There is nothing this country cannot do."

"You guys?" said Riley. "I meant the Underground Surveyor Apparatus."

"Oh," said Jamal. "*That* USA."

Riley turned to the head of his own personal Geek Squad. "Jake?"

"Well, even though it may look like one, the USA is definitely not your typical beachcombing metal detector. In fact, Dad's lab was testing it for the Army Corps of Engineers because they need to know what's waiting for them underground before they build a bridge or a dam or whatever."

"What is this USA thingamajiggereedoo?" asked Briana.

"You could call it a portable underground radar unit with Audio Response Targeting for heads-up detection and rapid target and depth estimation."

"Oh-kay," said Briana. "I'll call it that."

"It's perfect for pinpointing tunnels, treasure, utilities—all sorts of underground anomalies. You can actually *see* what's buried under the dirt."

"Including whatever Xylodyne may have buried

under the ninth hole," said Riley. "Do you know how to operate the underground radar?"

"Not yet," said Jake. "But I can learn. We still have the user's manual."

"Mongo?"

"Yeah."

"We need to borrow that gold coin collection your grandfather gave you."

"Again?"

"You'll get it back. Just like last time."

"Will it help Mr. Sowicky get his job back *and* save the fish?"

"Yes."

"Okay!"

"Thanks, big guy. Jamal?"

"What do you need, Riley Mack?"

"A little sleight of hand."

Jamal pulled a silver dollar out of Briana's ear.

"Would you puh-leeeze stop doing that?" she groaned.

"Not if the team needs me to do it for Operation Mulligan."

"Briana?" said Riley.

"Yeah?"

"First, we need some kind of security guard uniform for Mongo."

"Easy. We have that police officer Halloween costume he wore in the Unscrupulous-Candy-Store Sting. It's in storage at my house."

"Perfect. Can you give it a shoulder patch with the Xylodyne Dynamics logo?"

"Done. I'll download the graphic off their website."

"Excellent. Can you also mock up this?" Riley handed her a sheet of paper with scribbles on it.

"Is this like a treasure map?"

"Yeah. But make it look more high tech. Work in the topographical map elements and contour lines. Give it the Xylodyne logo, too."

"When do you need the finished document?"

"Tomorrow morning." Now he handed her two more sheets of paper. "These are your scripts. Get familiar with the first one. Record the second."

Briana glanced at the first script, studied the second. "You going for an authoritarian voice in script two, right? The kind of guy who won't take no for an answer?"

"Exactly."

"Easy-peasy. I'll lay it down on a handheld digital recorder, so we can use it in the field."

"Works for me."

"Oh, you know what? We should blast this through the bullhorn or my *poolside* karaoke machine."

"Dag, girl," said Jamal. "How many karaoke contests did you win?"

"Just one. But the prizes were fantabulous! And guys?"

"Yeah?" said Riley.

"I should probably block out a little time before Saturday to rehearse for the big show."

"Take whatever you need."

"Okay. How about another month?"

"You don't need that much rehearsal," said Riley. "You're already amazing."

"Easy for you to say. You're not the one rapping in a granny getup."

"For which," said Jamal, "we are all glad."

Riley turned to Jake. "Can you figure out how to run that underground radar machine by ten tomorrow morning?"

"I have a high degree of certainty in that regard."

"Um, is that a yes?"

"Yes."

"And how are we doing on GPS tracking devices?"

Jake swiveled in his chair and opened up a steel filing cabinet. "We still have three in storage."

"Bring one tomorrow."

"Will do."

"Mongo? Jamal needs to practice with your gold

coins before tomorrow morning."

"I'll run home and get them right away. They're hidden in my secret shoebox. The one on the top shelf of my bedroom closet."

Riley turned to Jamal. "Can you do that coin-pulling stunt out of a hole in the ground instead of a hole in somebody's head?"

"Sure."

"Good. Mongo, Jake, and Briana—we'll head up to the eighteenth hole at ten a.m. tomorrow morning."

"Why the *eighteenth* hole?" asked Briana.

"That's where Larry and Curly are working, remember?"

"Ri-i-i-ight."

"Am I with you guys, too?" asked Jamal.

"No. You'll hang back at the ninth hole. Here's your script. There's a fake fight in it."

"All right. Fisticuffs!"

"Be sure you bring your cell. When Briana gives the word, you'll sneak up the blind side of the hill and start digging in the sand trap with a toy shovel and bucket."

"How come?"

"Because, according to the treasure map Briana's working up for us, the ninth hole is where Mr. Paxton buried all of his gold!"

EARLY FRIDAY, RILEY AND HIS whole crew crammed into Mongo's golf cart and, once again, scooted through the hedges to avoid the country club's main gate.

"We'll swing by the ninth hole and drop off Jamal first," said Riley, steering the bouncing buggy onto the cart path. "Jamal? You've got your backstory down?"

"Yes. I may, however, embellish it slightly."

"Just make it real," said Briana. "Acting is believing!"

"Oh, I believe," said Jamal, "I believe I have heard you say that line before. Several times."

Riley took his foot off the accelerator and brought the quiet little cart to a stop.

Jamal hopped out, pressing his Bluetooth into his

ear, powering up his cell phone.

"Mongo?" said Riley. "Sand bucket and shovel."

Mongo, who was really too huge to ride in golf carts, handed Jamal his baby sister's beach toys. "Here you go."

"Thanks," said Jamal. "What do I owe you for it?" He plucked a shiny gold coin out of thin air.

"Careful," suggested Jake. "That single American Eagle Gold Bullion Coin was worth fifteen hundred dollars this morning."

"Your grandfather gave you a coin collection worth thirty-six thousand dollars?" Jamal asked.

"It's for my college education," Mongo said.

Jamal shook his head. "All my grandfather ever gave me was a couple Butter Rum Life Savers. They had lint on them, man. Pocket lint."

"I'll buy you a whole roll if we pull this thing off," said Riley.

"For real?"

"Yeah. Hang here. We'll be back in less than thirty minutes with Larry and Curly."

"Stik-O-Pep."

"Huh?"

"I like Stik-O-Pep way more than Butter Rum."

"Good to know. Now go hide in the woods until Briana calls."

"Right."

Jamal jogged to the tree line, gold coins jingling in his cargo shorts the whole way.

"Next stop, the eighteenth hole." Riley stomped on the accelerator, cut the steering wheel hard to the right, went off the cart path, and whirred across the fairway, heading for the far forest.

Fortunately, the Brookhaven Golf Course was still officially closed for renovations. There were no other golfers out on the fairway to yell at Riley for cutting doughnuts in their beautifully manicured grass.

"Um, wh-wh-where are we g-g-going, Riley?" asked Briana, hanging on for dear life in the bucking backseat.

"The eighteenth hole is on the far side of those trees. Jake? You ready to rock?"

"A-a-a-ffirmative," Jake stammered as the cart jounced across the bumpy grass. He was wearing a pretty heavy backpack loaded down with the underground radar gear and a laptop computer, all of it connected via thick cable to a flat metal dish attached to the end of a four-foot pole. When Jake slipped on his headphones, he looked exactly like the minesweeper in a bag of green army men.

Riley eased off the power as the cart puttered into a patch of woods.

"We'll ditch the cart here for now. Briana? Stand by."

"Standing by."

Mongo raised his hand.

"Yes, Mongo?"

"What am I supposed to do?"

Riley nodded toward the flapping flag of the eighteenth hole, barely fifty feet away. Larry and Curly were already on the far side of the green with their backhoe, dumping sand onto a patch of dirt that was about to become the final sand trap on the Brookhaven course. Both men were in their navy blue jumpsuits and yellow hardhats.

"Your mission, Mongo, should you choose to accept it, is to be much, much bigger than either of those two construction workers."

"I accept!" Mongo said eagerly.

"I hoped you would. Because we also need you to hide *this* underneath the seat of that backhoe."

Riley handed Mongo a real-time GPS tracking device. Since the high-tech gizmo wasn't much bigger than a paperclip, it practically disappeared in the palm of Mongo's humongous hand.

"There's double-sided foam tape on the back," Riley explained. "Just peel off the paper and slap it into place when nobody's looking."

"Okay. But, Riley?"

"Yeah?"

"When won't they be looking?"

Riley grinned. "When they're busy looking at me

and my map or Jake and his underground radar gear."

"Gotcha!"

"Jake?"

Jake raised up an ear cup. "Yeah?"

"Let's roll."

"Good luck, you guys," said Briana, pulling out a pair of binoculars, aiming them at Riley.

Riley tapped the side of his nose. "Wait for my signal."

Briana waggled the binoculars up and down.

Riley, Mongo, and Jake walked out of the woods, heading for the eighteenth hole.

"Hunker down, guys," Riley whispered.

They all hunched forward and duckwalked across the rough onto the shorter grass behind the eighteenth hole.

"Radar scan is coming in loud and clear," Jake whispered.

Riley peered over Jake's shoulder. In the small video monitor at the top of the handheld sensor, he saw what was buried under the eighteenth hole rough.

Nothing unusual.

"They laid in drainpipes and a layer of gravel," whispered Jake. "Other than that, the subterranean strata situation is pretty much what you'd expect. Sod, organic material, rock. Sprinkler pipes."

"I didn't think we'd find anything buried back here,"

said Riley, as quietly as he could. "The construction guys said they'd wrapped up the landfill project weeks ago. So if this was the last hole they were working on, chances are, they didn't bury anything under it."

Riley led the way as the threesome trudged across a shallow sand trap and started up the steeply sloped side of the small mesa that was the eighteenth hole green. As he neared the crest, Riley reached into his back pocket and pulled out his copy of the official-looking Xylodyne Dynamics treasure map Briana had worked up on her computer.

"Okay, you guys. It's showtime."

RILEY, MONGO, AND JAKE STEPPED up onto the neatly trimmed grass of the green.

Riley saw Larry seated in the elevated cab of the backhoe, about to dump another load of sugary white sand.

Larry saw Riley, too.

"Curly?" he shouted as he shut down his growling machinery. "Curly?"

Curly toddled up over the lip of the ridge holding a menacing sand rake.

Riley didn't flinch. "Oh," he said, quite casually. "It's you two."

Mongo straightened his back and linked his hands

together to crack a couple knuckles. At six two and 250 pounds, he towered over stout Curly and itty-bitty Larry.

"You're the hippy freak's nephew," said Larry, climbing out of the backhoe cab backward, like a toddler trying to dismount a merry-go-round.

"That's right," said Riley.

"Who are these other two?"

"My friends."

"What are youse kids doing out here?" demanded Curly. "This is a restricted-type area back here."

"Yeah. We know. And we know why."

"Huh?"

"Never mind," said Riley. "You guys work for *him*."

"Him who?" demanded Larry.

"Prescott Paxton!" Riley dramatically flapped open his fake map.

"What's that?"

"This? Nothing." He turned to Jake. "Try right here."

"You got it, boss." Jake swept the radar dish back and forth across the putting green so it hovered inches above the bristly blades.

"What's he doing?" shouted Larry.

As the two construction workers focused on Jake, Mongo made his way down to the backhoe perched on the lip of the sand pit.

"That's for me to know and you to find out," said Riley.

"Is that so?" said Curly. He raised his rake.

"Whoa. Settle down," said Riley, shooting up both of his hands. "Remember: anger is one letter short of danger."

"What's on that piece of paper?"

Riley shot a quick look from one thug to the other just in time to see Mongo stick the GPS tracker under the backhoe's seat.

"You heard my friend, kid," said Larry. "What's on that paper?"

"What paper?"

"The one in your freaking hands!" shouted Curly, raising his rake again.

Mongo hiked back up the hill to grab the tool on the backswing. He plucked it away.

"Play nice. You could put someone's eye out with this thing."

"Gimme back my rake, you big galoot!"

"Not until you prove to me that you know how to use it."

"That's it," squealed Larry. "We're callin' the cops. Youse kids are trespassing here."

"Hey, take it easy," said Riley. "We're willing to share."

"Share?"

"Sure. From what Sara says, there's enough buried out here for everybody."

"Not here though," reported Jake as he flicked a switch to make his radar gear beep and blip like an incoming UFO.

"What's that nerd doin' with that metal detector?" insisted Larry.

"It's not a metal detector," explained Jake. "It's underground radar gear." He turned to Riley. "There's nothing here worth digging up."

Riley consulted his map. "You think this intel is bad?"

"Might be."

"Give me that map!" Larry snatched the paper out of Riley's hands. "Hey, Curly—check it out. There's a Xylodyne logo on this thing."

Curly shuffled over and read the title printed across the top: "Retrievables Recovery Plan."

"Darn it!" Riley said to Jake. "Sara promised us."

"Who's Sara?" asked Larry.

"Mr. Paxton's daughter."

"The bratty blond?"

"You've met her?"

"She dropped by the construction site once or twice to poke fun at us," said Curly, making a face like he was remembering the time he accidentally ate dog poop.

"Called us Munchkins," said Larry.

"Garden gnomes," added Curly.

"Shorty McShorts' Shorts."

Riley pretended to be shocked. "No! How come?"

"We're short, kid. Vertically challenged."

"But that don't mean we like hearing about it," said Curly.

"Of course not," said Riley. "Well, anyway, Sara is mad at her father. She wanted a flock of doves to fly in and land on her arms when she sings her big number at the talent show tomorrow night."

Curly nodded. "Sure. Like in Vegas."

"I guess. But, Mr. Paxton, he's all worried about the health code, so he won't let her rent the trained birds. To get back at him, Sara stole this treasure map out of his briefcase."

"Treasure?"

"Yeah. Her father buried a ton of gold coins underneath the ninth hole. But now . . ." Riley flapped a hand toward Jake. "The radar says there's nothing here."

"The *ninth* hole?" said Larry.

"Yeah."

"Kid? You know how to read?"

"Sure."

"What's that flag say?"

"Nine."

"Try again, Einstein."

"Nine," said Riley. "Because one plus eight equals nine."

"That's an eighteen!"

"Huh?"

"A one next to an eight? That's eighteen! No wonder Korea's beating America on all them math scores."

"We're on the wrong hole?" said Jake.

"I guess," said Riley.

"This 'Retrievables Recovery Plan,'" Curly said to Larry as they both studied Briana's topographical masterpiece, "means Mr. Paxton was planning on coming back to *retrieve* all them sacks we buried in the so-called landfill for him!"

Score, thought Riley. *We have confirmation.*

Mr. Paxton had definitely buried *something* underneath the golf course.

Riley touched the side of his nose. His cue to Briana.

"That no-good weasel," said Larry. "If we knew what was inside them black trash bags we was burying . . ."

Riley's cell phone started chirping.

"That's Sara's ringtone," he said, putting the phone to his ear. "Hello? What? No way! Jamal Wilson? Thanks for the heads up!" He thumbed the off button and slid the phone back into his pocket. "Come on, you guys. Sara's up at the country club. She just saw Jamal Wilson heading for the ninth hole!"

"Whoa," shouted Larry. "Not so fast. Who's this Jamal Wilson individual?"

"Our competition. He's already out there—stealing our gold!"

RILEY LED THE MAD DASH back to the golf cart.

Mongo, Jake, Larry, and Curly were right behind him.

"We have a cart stashed in the woods!" Riley shouted over his shoulder.

"Good!" said Larry, who was huffing and puffing ten yards back.

Curly was having an even harder time running and breathing at the same time. Both construction workers were totally out of shape.

Riley reached the forest first and had a few seconds to check in with Briana.

"Did you cue Jamal?" he asked.

"Right after we hung up."

"Cool. Okay, we'll meet you back at Jake's place in like an hour."

"I'll record that security-guard track you need for later."

"Awesome. And Bree?"

"Yeah?"

"Thanks!"

She shot Riley a wink and took off through the trees.

Riley hopped into the golf cart and turned the key. He figured he'd drive down and pick up the adults.

It'd be faster than waiting for them to run up the hill or have a heart attack—whichever came first.

"You see," said Jake, "gold is the one sure investment."

"I know," said Larry, who had squeezed into the backseat of the golf cart with Jake and Curly. "I seen ads on TV."

"So," asked Curly, "how'd this Jamal character get his hands on Mr. Paxton's treasure map?"

"He stole it!" blurted Mongo, riding up front in the passenger seat. Mongo sounded nervous because he hated it when a plan included him having to memorize lines.

"Jamal," Mongo said, taking it from the top a second time. "The map. He stole it. From Sara."

"At the copy shop," prompted Riley.

"At the coffee shop!" said Mongo. "I will pound him."

"Not if I get my hands on him first!" said Larry.

"Yeah, we're the ones who buried the gold," added Curly. "Diggers keepers, losers weepers!"

Oh-kay. Riley had never heard that particular spin on the phrase before.

He nudged Mongo with his knee.

"No! Jamal. Is. Mine!" Mongo turned to glare at the two construction workers.

Larry and Curly held up their hands.

"Whoa. Take it easy, big fellow," said Larry.

"We don't mean no disrespect here," echoed Curly.

Riley patted Mongo on the knee to let his friend know he could relax. His scripted lines were over.

"Hang on to your hardhats, everybody," said Riley, steering the cart off the path and into the forest fringing the ninth hole. "I'm ditching the cart. We don't want anybody up at the club sticking their noses into our business."

As the cart careened across the rough, Larry and Curly held on to their jouncing yellow helmets. Riley glanced to the right and saw Jamal using his plastic sand bucket and shovel to send up a cloud of gritty dust. His actions in the sand trap were hidden from the clubhouse by the grassy knoll of the elevated hole.

Riley slammed on the brakes. Mongo bounded out of the cart.

"I'm gonna lay down the hurt!" Arms flailing, he

raced toward the sand trap.

"Let's go cream this Jamal kid," said Larry after he and Curly had crawled out of the cart.

Riley placed a hand on the short man's shoulder. "Give Mongo a minute." He head-gestured toward the ninth hole.

Larry and Curly looked over. All they could see were puffs of sand being flung up from the sunken pit.

"Where's Mongo?"

"My guess?" said Riley. "On top of Jamal. Pummeling him."

In truth, Riley knew that both Mongo and Jamal were currently lying on their backs, tossing fistfuls of sand into the air to make it look like they were furiously fighting.

"Your friend Mongo. He has anger issues. Am I right?"

"Big-time. Jake? Grab your gear. It's time to check out the mother lode."

When they reached the sand trap, Mongo had Jamal pinned flat on his back.

"Get off me, you boorish bruiser!" said Jamal, kicking and squirming.

"Hello, Wilson," said Riley, straddling the edge of the sand trap with his arms akimbo.

"Riley Mack?" said Jamal, pretending to be terrified.

"In the flesh. I understand you took something that didn't belong to you."

"Ha! Says who?"

"Sara Paxton."

Larry strutted forward to sneer down at Jamal. "We hear you stole her daddy's treasure map outta the coffee shop."

Jamal glanced at Riley.

Riley made a face to say, *Go with it.*

"Yeah, that's right. I boosted it while she was enjoying a grande mocha latte with double whip." Jamal stood and dusted himself off.

A shiny gold coin fell out of his hand.

"What's that?" said Curly.

Mongo snatched the gold piece off the ground. "An American Eagle Gold coin!"

"Where'd you find it, Jamal?" said Riley.

"Down that hole." He flexed out the fingers on both his hands, the way a magician does to prove he has nothing up his sleeve. Then he reached into the two-foot deep pit. "Here's another one."

Yep. Instead of pulling a coin out of an ear, he pulled it out of the sand.

"Jake?" said Riley. "Scan the sand trap. Record the visual on digital."

"On it," said Jake.

"So, Wilson—any more gold down in that hole?" asked Riley.

"Probably," said Jamal. "See, my father, Ahab, he's in the treasure-reclamation business. He always says, 'Son, where you find one gold coin, you'll find another.' Why, I remember deep-sea diving in the Bermuda Triangle, searching for sunken treasure near the wreckage of a Spanish galleon, the HMS *Pinafore*. The shark-infested waters were murky . . ."

Riley glanced at his watch. He knew Jamal could go on for hours.

"How about *this* hole? Any more gold in this hole?"

"Hand me my sand bucket and I'll show you."

Riley tossed the bright-red bucket over to Jamal, who proceeded to reach down into the hole a dozen more times and plunk a dozen gold coins in the plastic bucket.

"That's it," said Jamal. "That's all the coins that floated up to the surface after we had all those heavy rains."

Riley waited for just a second.

He wanted to make sure that Larry and Curly were dumb enough to believe gold could float.

Yep. They were.

Neither one of them said a word. They just stood there nodding like Bob the Builder bobblehead dolls.

But Riley could tell: their mental wheels were spinning. The two construction workers were trying to figure out how they could dig up the ninth hole and steal all the gold—*for themselves!*

"LOOKS LIKE XYLODYNE BURIED A bunch of stuff right here," said Jake, as he held the radar disc over the sand trap.

Riley glanced over at Larry and Curly. The two men were keeping mum. Pouting out their lower lips. Sniffing. Twitching.

Yep. Another confirmation. They knew *exactly* where they had buried a big stack of whatever toxic chemicals Mr. Paxton and Xylodyne didn't want anybody to know about.

Jake's radar gear was blipping and blooping. "It almost looks like a pile of plastic garbage bags stacked on top of one another, maybe six feet below the surface."

"I bet all those garbage bags are stuffed with gold coins!" said Jamal.

Larry turned to Curly. "That's why those sacks were so freaking heavy!"

"Shhh!" said Curly. Shaking his head. Miming for Larry to dummy up.

"This is fantastic!" said Riley. "We should come back, late at night, when it's too dark for the country-club security cameras to see what we're doing!"

Larry and Curly probably didn't realize it, but they were both nodding.

"You guys could do the digging with your backhoe," Riley said. "But you'll need short people to crawl down into the hole to retrieve the gold."

Now Larry and Curly were nodding *and* smiling.

They had both just realized that, for the first time in their lives, being small would be a big advantage.

"That's where we come in," said Riley. "You dig. We climb down and mine for gold. We split everything, fifty-fifty."

"You're clever, kid," said Larry.

"Thanks. So do we have a deal?"

"What about all them gold coins in the sand bucket?" said Curly.

"Those are mine!" said Mongo.

"My friend is correct," said Riley. "Since you gentlemen were in no way responsible for the retrieval of these particular assets, you are not entitled to that fifty-fifty split, which we were discussing for all *future* extractions."

"Sure, kid," said Curly. "Seems fair. Right, Larry?"

"Sure, sure. No problem."

Riley knew they were pretending to play along, but secretly itching for the kids to leave.

Larry cocked a thumb toward Jamal. "Shouldn't youse three take this Jamal character somewheres quiet and work him over so he don't blab about our plan to *his* sidekicks?"

"You're right! Mongo? Haul Jamal and that bucket of gold coins back to the golf cart. Jake? Take a reading on top of the green. We may want to dig it up later, too."

"On it," said Jake as he lugged his gear up the embankment.

"Now, excavating the hole, itself, undetected, that'll be a tall order. But I have an idea how—"

"Everybody down!" shouted Jake.

He leaped off the elevated green and landed hard in the sand trap.

"Jake? What's wrong?" asked Riley melodramatically.

"I think somebody saw me!"

"Where?"

"The country club. People are on the deck, eating lunch."

Riley punched a fist into his palm. "I knew it! This is why we need to do this operation under the cloak of darkness! Okay, everybody. Keep calm. I'll call Sara. She's our eyes and ears on the inside."

"Where is she?" asked Larry.

"On that deck having lunch." Riley pulled out his cell. "Gosh darn it all!"

"What's the matter, now, kid?" asked Curly.

"My phone battery is dead. And we need to call Sara *right away* to see if we're busted. What if her dad is with her and saw us snooping around where he hid all his gold?"

"That would not be good." Curly dug a cell phone out of his coveralls. "Here. Use mine."

"Thanks!"

Riley thumbed in a number, fast.

Jake's cell phone rang.

"Hello?" said Jake.

"Jake?" said Riley.

"Yeah."

"Sorry, wrong number."

"No problem. You want Sara's? I have it in my phone-book."

Jake started pressing buttons on his phone, pretending to be searching through his directory. In fact, he was recording the number of his most recent incoming call. "Got it," he said, meaning he now had *Curly's*

214

cell phone number recorded and saved.

"That's okay," said Riley, pressing another string of digits on Curly's phone. "You're four-four-five-*two*, Sara is four-four-five-*three*."

"Correct."

"Okay. Hang on."

He pretended to wait for Sara to answer. In truth, he had just called his own cell phone, which was powered off and in his pocket.

"Sara? Riley. Yeah. No, we took care of Jamal. Look— we're behind the ninth hole now and I made a mistake. I sent Jake up to scout out the green. Did anybody see him? No? You're sure? Awesome. Thanks, Sara. Don't worry. We're going to teach your father a lesson he'll never forget. I don't know. Maybe tonight. I have to check with our partners. Two guys. Look Sara, I had to. They have the machinery we need to dig up the gold. Right. You, too."

Riley pressed the OFF button and fidgeted with the phone as he pretended to admire it. "Is this one of those press-to-talk walkie-talkie phones?"

"Yeah."

"Cool."

Riley was actually using the time to erase any record of his outgoing call—just in case Curly was smart enough to check to see whose number Riley had actually dialed.

215

He handed the phone back to Curly. "That was close. *Too* close." He dragged his foot across the sand to fill in the hole Jamal had dug. "Let's meet up here again tonight. Actually, tomorrow morning would be better. Like two or three a.m. You guys bring the backhoe and . . ."

Larry was shaking his head.

Curly was smiling. "Why the rush, kid?"

"Huh?"

"What you're suggesting," said Larry, "would not be prudent."

"Or wise, neither," added Curly.

"We should wait," said Larry. "Until after the big reopening."

"Definitely," said Curly. "Best to wait at least a week. Maybe a month."

"But, what if Mr. Paxton comes back before then to retrieve all his coins?"

"Not gonna happen, kid," said Larry. "Otherwise, why'd he have us bury the gold in the first place?"

"You're right! That's smart thinking."

"I know. But, then again, I'm an adult."

"Okay. We'll do it your way. It's like I always say: grown-ups know best!"

OF COURSE, RILEY KNEW LARRY and Curly wouldn't wait.

They'd do just as he suggested and head back to the ninth hole sand trap at two or three in the morning.

That's why he and Jake were spending the night at Mongo's house.

And why they had slapped that GPS tracker in the cab of the backhoe.

They took turns sleeping. Two guys would snooze; the third would eat Doritos and keep an eye on the laptop computer tracking the backhoe's location.

At 2:45 a.m., Jake nudged Riley and Mongo awake.

"The mole is on the move," he whispered.

Jake and Riley had unrolled their sleeping bags on the floor of Mongo's bedroom, which was decorated with all sorts of teddy bears, not that anybody would ever tease the big guy about it. Well, at least not twice.

Riley took a minute to yawn, rub the sleep out of his eyes, and pop a breath mint.

Mongo did not.

"Okay," said Riley, turning to Mongo, whose security uniform looked a little wrinkled, because he'd figured it would be easier if he just slept in his costume. "You've got the go bag?"

"Check," said Mongo through a yawn that smelled a lot like the onion rings and chili dogs he'd had for dinner the night before. He hoisted his heavy backpack filled with gear off the floor.

Riley's backpack was empty. They needed it to carry out whatever they found buried underneath the ninth hole.

"Give Briana her wake-up call," Riley said to Jake. "We'll contact her as soon as we have what we need."

Fifteen minutes later, Riley and Mongo were on their bellies behind the ninth hole watching Larry and Curly scooping out the sand trap with their backhoe.

Riley flipped down his father's old night-vision goggles so he could see everything clear as day (except that it was all extremely green).

Larry was up in the cab, working the twin sticks controlling the boom and bucket. Curly was down by the hole with a shovel.

"How far down do you think they've dug?" asked Mongo.

"Hang on." Riley adjusted the zoom on his goggles. "Okay. Curly is signaling to Larry to cut the engine."

In the distance, the backhoe engine shuddered to a halt.

"Now Curly is jumping into the ditch. I can't see the top of his helmet, so I guess they're down five, maybe six feet. Okay. This is it. Curly's waving his shovel out of the hole. He's found something."

Mongo stood up. Dusted off his pants. Tugged down on the brim of his costume cop hat.

Riley moved the digital recorder closer to the bullhorn, then aimed a battery-powered spotlight straight at the backhoe.

"You ready?" he asked Mongo.

"Ready."

Riley flicked on the switch to the 4,200-lumen searchlight. Its beacon was about as bright as the one in a lighthouse.

Next, he pulled the trigger on the bullhorn and pressed PLAY on the recorder.

"Freeze!" boomed Briana's digitally altered, Darth Vader–esque voice. "This is Brookhaven Security! Do not move!"

Riley pressed PAUSE as Curly climbed out of the hole. Then he and Larry did as the voice had commanded.

Now Mongo swaggered into the dusty beam of the searchlight, swinging his plastic nightstick.

Riley punched PLAY.

"And don't think you can outrun our guard," Briana's robo-voice continued. "Just because Officer Pettigrew had his appendix removed last week doesn't mean he can't chase after you two."

Riley hit PAUSE.

Curly and Larry looked at each other.

Made up their minds.

And took off running.

Riley hit PLAY one more time.

"Wait!" shouted the bullhorn voice. "Come back, you two. Are you okay, Officer Pettigrew?"

"No," groaned Mongo. "My stitches. I think I popped my stitches."

Riley followed Curly and Larry with the handheld spotlight until they disappeared into the forest on the far side of the fairway.

He doused the lamp. "Good work, Mongo!"

"Did I do the stitches line right?"

"Perfect." Riley slipped on a pair of heavy work gloves. "Come on. We need to check out that hole. Now!"

They dashed across the damp grass to the sand trap. Riley handed Mongo his empty backpack.

"I'm going in." He hopped down into the six-foot-deep hole and switched on his flashlight.

"What is it?" asked Mongo, who was peering down into the pit.

"Can't tell yet."

Riley saw all sorts of torn black bags, their outsides stained with white smears. Clearly, the trash can liners weren't waterproof. The top one was punctured in several places as if rodents had nibbled through the plastic. Chalky chemicals had leaked out and polluted the groundwater.

Riley reached into the top bag and felt some kind of lumpy sack. He moved his flashlight closer and, inside the trash bag, saw several brown paper bags stacked on top of one another.

"It's flour. No, wait." He ran the beam of his flashlight along the very generic lettering on the outside of the paper bag:

Protein-Power Pancake Mix

10 Pounds

U.S. Government Property

For Dining Facility Use Only

Commercial Resale Is Unlawful.

Product of Mobile Meal Manufacturing

"It's some kind of government-surplus pancake mix."

"Just grab it and let's go!" said Mongo.

He was right. They could examine the evidence later. Right now, they needed to alert Briana because she needed to make another phone call as Mr. Paxton, this time to Curly's cell.

"Here!" Riley tossed the ten-pound sack out of the hole. Mongo jammed it inside Riley's empty backpack. Then he reached down into the trench, grabbed Riley by the arm, and hauled him up and out.

"We need to pack our gear and leave," said Riley.

"What about the hole?"

"Curly and Larry will be back to fill it in as soon as Mr. Paxton calls them!"

They dashed back toward the treeline.

"I'll take care of our junk," said Mongo. "You call Briana."

"Works for me."

RILEY LISTENED IN VIA THREE-WAY conference as Briana placed the call.

"Hello?" he heard a nervous Curly say.

"Are you the idiot they call Curly?"

"Who is this?

"Prescott P. Paxton. I believe we've met?"

"Yes, sir."

"Curly, you may wonder why a very important man such as myself is calling you at three thirty in the morning."

"Well, yeah, sort of. How'd you even get my phone number?"

"I'm filthy rich. I can get anything I want or need, Mr. Curly."

Riley cringed. They totally should've found out Curly's last name or even his *real* first name.

"Yes, sir, sir," said Curly, clearly cowed by the early-morning phone call from the chairman and CEO of Xylodyne Dynamics. "Um, can I help you with something, sir?"

"*Nyes.* The Brookhaven Country Club security patrol just called. Apparently, someone matching your description was seen with another short, stout fellow running a backhoe out behind hole number nine of our beautifully refurbished golf course."

"Yeah," said Curly. "That was me and Larry."

"What, pray tell, were you and this Larry chap doing with a backhoe at this early hour?"

"You really want to know?"

"*Nyes.*"

"Digging up your freaking gold!"

Briana paused perfectly. "You know . . . about . . . my . . . gold?"

Okay. Now she was laying it on a little thick.

"Yeah, pal. We know everything. See, we got our hands on your little treasure map. The one your daughter stole out of your briefcase and copied at the coffee shop."

"I see. Very well, Curly. You and your chum seem to have me over a barrel, as they say."

"Yeah. We do."

"Does anybody else know about our little landfill?"

"Just some punk kids who were nosing around the golf course earlier. Me and Larry scared 'em off."

Riley grinned. *Oh they did, did they?*

"Well done. Was one of the boys, perchance, an impudent young African American by the name of Jamal Wilson?"

"Yeah. He was there."

"Oh, dear."

"What's the matter?"

"Mr. Wilson's father is a world-renowned treasure hunter."

"Yeah. We heard about that. How they went scuba diving in the Bermuda Triangle and all."

"We need to move quickly."

"How come?"

"If we don't, Jamal's father will."

"What do you mean?"

"He's a pro! Ahab Wilson is the man who, single-handedly, dug up Blackbeard's gold on the Isle of Tortuga!"

"So what do you suggest we do here, Mr. Paxton?"

"First, go back to that sand trap and fill in your hole. Put everything back the way it was."

"No problem."

"Then, tonight, while we're holding the gala reopening bash in the ballroom, you and your friend return to the sand trap and dig it up again. The talent show will be the perfect cover. I'll make sure all the security guards are inside, protecting our special guests and dignitaries. We'll turn up the music and drown out any noise you two might make with your heavy machinery while digging up the gold."

"And why, exactly, would we want to do that?"

"Did I forget to mention that I would give you fifty percent of everything you retrieve?"

"We want sixty."

"Oh, you do, do you?"

"But we'll settle for fifty."

"Good. Do we have a deal?"

"Yes, sir, Mr. Paxton."

"Excellent."

"So, tell me: how much loot are we talking about?"

"At today's market price for gold? Sixty million dollars!"

Curly whistled in astonishment.

"*Nyes.* We'll make the split Sunday afternoon in your construction trailer."

"Okey-doke."

"One more thing, Curly."

"What's that?"

"As you may know, Xylodyne Dynamics has extensive contacts within the United States military establishment."

"So?"

"So, if you and your friend Larry try to double-cross me, if you attempt to abscond with my gold coins or dig them up *before* tomorrow night, a team of navy SEALs and Green Berets will hunt you down and eliminate you with extreme prejudice. Do I make myself clear?"

"Yes, sir."

"Good! Now go fill in that hole!"

"Right away, sir."

Riley powered off his phone to make sure the conference call was disconnected. Then he speed-dialed Briana.

"How was I?" she gushed.

"Perfect. Your best performance ever!"

"Really?"

"Totally. Go back to sleep. You need your rest. Tomorrow night's your big night."

"What're you guys doing next?"

"In the morning, we'll go see Ms. Kaminski."

"The science teacher? Why?"

"We need her to check out a sack of pancake powder."

* * *

Saturday was an extremely busy day.

Briana needed to rehearse her act for the talent show finals. (She called Riley three times to let him know how nervous she was.)

Riley's mom wanted him to make sure his sport coat still fit for their big night as the country club's guests of honor. He also had to go see Ms. Kaminski at the Fairview Civic Center, where she'd be spending her day off at a CSI Fan Fest.

So at noon, when his mother went to her office to take care of some paperwork, Riley biked to the civic center. Ms. Kaminski was with a group of people in the parking lot, looking at a car parked behind yellow police tape. There were bullet-hole decals on the window and a dead mannequin sitting behind the steering wheel.

"Ms. Kaminski?" said Riley.

"Oh, hi, Riley. Give me a second. I need to work out my trajectory angles. Whoever comes up with the best solution to this staged crime scene wins a souvenir CSI tote bag!"

"Cool. But, well—we think we found what's killing all those fish."

"You identified the source of contamination?"

"We think so. And it's not just Mongo's fishpond that's polluted. It's the whole watershed."

"Did you guys alert the EPA?"

"Not yet. First we want to make sure we know what kind of poison we're talking about."

He held up a plastic baggie filled with a cup of the grainy powder he had scooped out of the ten-pound paper sack.

"What is it?"

"Pancake mix. We found it buried under the Brookhaven Golf Course."

"Who would bury pancake mix?"

"I don't know. But, there's tons of the stuff buried out there."

"Really?"

"Yeah."

"Wow. A *real* crime to solve. Mr. Mack, do you have time to come with me to my boyfriend's chemistry lab?"

"Yes, ma'am!"

Riley secured his bike to the rack on the back of Ms. Kaminski's small car.

"You know, Riley," she said as they drove away from the civic center, "you and Hubert really ought to work this up as a science project next year."

"We might. But first, we need to save some fish."

"THIS IS WORSE THAN CHINESE dog food," said Ms. Kaminski's boyfriend, Ron, after he ran a series of tests on the pancake powder.

"What'd you find?" asked Ms. Kaminski.

"Melamine *and* cyanuric acid. If this junk leached into the water table, it would explain why all those fish died."

"What exactly are melamine and cyanuric acid?" asked Riley.

"Melamine," said Ms. Kaminski, "is a chemical high in nitrogen that's used to make all kinds of plastics and fertilizers. It's also been helpful for synthesizing medicines and as a nitrogen supplement for dairy cows."

"But wouldn't it make the cows sick?"

"Not on its own," Ms. Kaminski said. "Melamine is essentially nontoxic. But combined with cyanuric acid . . ."

"KA-BOOM!" said Ron. "Mix the two, and the concoction causes crystals to form in urine, which can create kidney stones that lead to acute renal failure and death."

"Any other symptoms?" asked Riley. He was afraid he and Mongo might have contaminated themselves just by touching the leaky sack of pancake powder.

"Well, let's see," said Ron. "Vomiting. Lack of appetite. Sluggishness. Frequent urination and increased water intake. So, if your dog is spending all day at the water bowl . . ."

"But," said Riley, "this isn't dog food. It's pancake mix. Why would anybody want to put extra nitrogen in pancakes?"

"To fool food inspectors into thinking it was high in protein," explained Ms. Kaminski.

"The same reason a Chinese company put melamine and cyanuric acid in baby formula," said Ron. "See, they could add the cheap chemicals and some even cheaper water and maintain the protein level while reducing the actual milk contents. Less milk in the milk powder meant more money in their pockets."

Riley suddenly realized what was going on. "The label on the bag where we found the powder, it said 'Protein-Power Pancake Mix.'"

"There you go," said Ron. "Somebody was attempting to run the same scam. They made it *look* like their product was packed with protein when, in fact, it was just loaded down with nitrogen."

"Because," said Ms. Kaminski, "the tests for protein content in food typically measure nitrogen levels, not actual protein."

"This is horrible," said Riley.

"Totally," said Ron.

"Where exactly did you find this pancake powder, Riley?" asked Ms. Kaminski.

He showed the science teacher and chemist a printout of the image Jake's underground radar had recorded during its scan of the sand trap.

"These shadows suggest bags piled on top of bags," said Ms. Kaminski. "Like you'd see in a warehouse."

"Do you know who made the pancake mix?" asked Ron.

"A company called Mobile Meal Manufacturing. There was a flag on the bag, too."

Ron turned to his computer. Clacked the keyboard. "Okay. Here we go: Mobile Meal Manufacturing is a subsidiary of Xylodyne Dynamics. Somebody probably found out about the elevated nitrogen in the pancake powder and decided they'd better bury the evidence."

"Why didn't they just burn it or something?" Ms. Kaminski wondered out loud.

"That'd be a pretty huge bonfire," said Ron as he turned back to his computer screen. "Uh-oh."

"What?" said Riley.

"This would explain that American flag you saw on the bag. According to their website, Mobile Meal Manufacturing is 'devoted to feeding our troops a little taste of home no matter how far from home duty may call.' They made this Protein-Power Pancake Mix for the United States military."

Riley remembered something else that was printed on the bag's label:

For Dining Facility Use Only.

Dining facility was the new term for what the army used to call the mess hall.

"They sold this poison to the army?" Riley mumbled in disbelief. "Ms. Kaminski?"

"Yes?"

"Can you take me home?"

"Well, sure, but don't you think we need to—"

"I need to call my dad. It's urgent."

"You can use my phone," said Ron.

"Not really. I have to do a video link over the internet. He's a soldier. Over in Afghanistan."

"Oh, my," said Ms. Kaminski. "Do you think he ate some of these poisoned pancakes?"

"I sure hope not. But I'm pretty sure some of his soldiers did!"

RILEY RACED THROUGH THE FRONT door.

"Hi, hon," said his mom. "Where you going in such a rush?"

"Um, just up to my room. I want to make sure my shirt isn't too wrinkled. For tonight."

"Well, if it is, bring it down and I'll iron it later. I have to run off to the hair salon with my coupon!"

"Have fun!"

"I always have fun when everything is free." His mom twirled her car keys on her finger. "Remember: we're leaving for the country club at six."

"I'll be ready. Hey, maybe you should go get that mani-pedi, too."

His mom looked at her fingernails. "Ooh. You're right. Okay, I'll be out for a couple hours. Can you stay out of trouble while I'm gone?"

"I can try."

That made his mom smile. "See you later, Riley."

"Later."

As soon as she was out the door, Riley raced up the steps to the second floor. He couldn't tell his mother what was going on. Not until his dad said it was okay. He had promised to keep her "out of the loop on all things Paxton." This bombshell would definitely ruin her big night at the country club.

He dashed into his room. Flipped open his laptop. It was 1:30 p.m., which meant that it was 10 p.m. in Afghanistan.

"Be there," Riley muttered as the computer made its transcontinental connection. "Be there!"

The video box opened.

"Good evening Mr. Mack."

It was Sergeant Lorincz.

"Hello, Sergeant. Is my dad available?"

"Negative."

"It's kind of urgent—"

"I'm sorry, Mr. Mack, but—"

"Hey, did any of your guys, the ones you said are sick, did any of them eat pancakes in the mess hall?"

"Pancakes?"

"Yes, sir. Made with Protein-Power Pancake Mix from a company called Mobile Meal Manufacturing?"

"It's a possibility," said Sergeant Lorincz. "Whenever we hit a base with a proper dining facility, a lot of the men go for hot grub like pancakes in the morning. Sure beats the MREs we eat in the field."

"Can you talk to the cooks or something? Find out what sort of mix they use when they make pancakes?"

The sergeant had an extremely quizzical look on his face.

"Sir, we found something. Something bad. See, we live near the headquarters for Xylodyne Dynamics and they own Mobile Meal Manufacturing and they've been putting bad junk in their pancake powder to fake out the food inspectors on the protein level."

"Come again?"

"This could be what's making your men sick. The symptoms you described, they're what would happen if you ate melamine and cyanuric acid."

"I see."

"It's what the Chinese did with that baby formula that got recalled, remember?"

"Yes . . ."

"So, maybe you and my dad could just make sure none of your guys have been exposed to . . ."

Sergeant Lorincz was shaking his head. "I'm afraid your father won't be able to help us out on this one,

Riley. About an hour ago, some MPs took him to Bagram Airfield. He's being detained."

"What?"

"They think your father made our men sick by engaging in what some desk jockey is calling 'risky humanitarian activities.'"

Riley remembered his dad telling him how he and his troops were visiting hospitals and teaching the locals how to play baseball.

"We visited several schools and hospitals over the past six months," the sergeant continued. "Spent time with the locals. Earned their trust. Now, the brass says that, by encouraging these efforts, your father recklessly exposed his troops to germs and disease."

"They think my dad made all those soldiers sick?"

"Roger that. They're conducting a hearing. First thing tomorrow. Oh-seven-hundred hours."

"Is it a court martial?"

"No. It's an inquiry. But, Riley?"

"Yes, sir?"

"They're holding your father in the brig overnight."

Riley swallowed hard.

He didn't need Jamal to tell him what *brig* meant.

It was the army word for jail.

RILEY CALLED HIS WHOLE CREW together for an emergency meeting at the Pizza Palace about "Operation Flapjack."

The five of them were seated in their regular booth near the back. Since it was 3:00 p.m., the lunch rush was over. That meant they could talk freely without anyone overhearing their conversation.

"I cannot believe the horriblelocity of this situation!" said Briana after Riley had filled his friends in on what was going on over in Afghanistan. "It just keeps getting worse and worse."

"And worse," added Mongo.

"What're we gonna do, Riley Mack?" asked Jamal. "Reassess, reevaluate, and revise?"

Riley shook his head. "No. We stick with the original plan. We have Larry and Curly dig up the evidence under the ninth hole during the talent show."

"And then we hit them with the portable floodlights," said Jake.

"Which I drag from behind the construction trailer," said Mongo, "and haul out to the fairway."

"Making sure you aim the lights at the ninth hole," added Riley.

"Right."

"But you don't turn them on until nine thirty p.m."

"Right. Does anybody have a watch I can borrow?"

Riley peeled his off his wrist. "Take mine. I'll use my cell phone. Timing is crucial on this one, guys. There is an eight-and-a-half–hour time difference between Fairview and Afghanistan. My dad's hearing starts at seven a.m. over there, which is . . ."

"Ten thirty p.m. here," said Jake, because he did math quicker than anyone at the table.

Riley turned to Briana. "You'll be backstage at the talent show."

"Right. I guess. Unless I go on last."

Riley shook his head. "You won't. Sara Paxton will."

"How come?"

"We need to make sure Mr. Paxton and his distinguished guests from the EPA and Pentagon don't skip out early."

"Cool."

"Once Mongo flips the switch on the spotlights . . ."

"I cause a commotion! I scream and, clutching both hands over my heart, shout, 'Look, everybody! They're digging up the golf course!'"

"I run to the window," said Jamal. "And say, 'She's right! They're digging up the golf course!'"

"And then," said Briana, "we both peer out the window and say something like, 'Is that poisoned army food? It looks like they're digging up poisoned army food!'"

"Which," said Jamal, "ticks off the army general. So, he goes running outside."

"Then," said Briana, "I win the talent show scholarship while the bad guys all go to jail for the rest of their lives and pay a bazillion dollars in EPA fines to clean up the creek." She turned to Riley and smiled. "That's basically the gist of it, right?"

"More or less," said Riley. "But we have to add in a new layer."

"Oooh. I *love* layers!"

"Jake? Can you hook me up with some kind of wireless video camera and then feed its video stream into an internet teleconference?"

"Sure," said Jake. "We'll borrow my dad's helmet cam. It has microwave picture transmission. I'll wire the receiver into your laptop via the USB port."

"Your father has a helmet cam?" said Jamal.

"Yeah. He bought it to record his downhill runs when he goes skiing. If, you know, he ever decides to go skiing."

"Excellent," said Riley. "Sergeant Lorincz is arranging things at the other end. We link up over the internet and feed the hearing all the evidence as it is being revealed and have General Clarke officially corroborate it. Briana?"

"Yeah?"

"When's dress rehearsal for the talent show?"

"In like an hour. Four o'clock. Then I have to get into my granny makeup. . . ."

Riley shook his head. "No you don't. Go with the 'Hallelujah' song from *Shrek*. We want you to win the scholarship."

All the guys were nodding in agreement.

"But," said Briana, "we told Mr. Paxton—"

"Mr. Paxton isn't one of the judges. Besides, by the end of the competition, he'll be the one in jail instead of my dad."

"Okay," said Briana. "That'll make things a little easier."

"Good. Now, at the dress rehearsal, I need you to do

some heavy-duty acting. I want Sara and that bunch to think we're having a huge fight."

"Um, okay. But why?"

"So they'll listen to me when I tell her how she can beat you."

Briana's eyes became sad and moist. "You're on *her* side? I can't believe this, Riley." A tear trickled down her cheek. "After all we've been through?"

Riley felt terrible. "No, Bree. It's just a scam. I need Sara to go last and to add something to her act."

Briana sobbed.

"I promise," said Riley. "I'm not really rooting for her to—"

"Psyche!" said Briana, smiling brightly. "Fooled you. I wasn't really crying, I was *acting!*" She pulled her hand down in front of her face and bowed her head like she was taking a curtain call.

"Wow," said Mongo, dabbing at his eyes with the back of his fist. "That was fake?"

"Yep."

"Fooled me. I thought my heart was gonna break."

"Me, too," said Jake.

"Not me, Bree," said Jamal, leaning back in the booth confidently. "See, I knew it was a sham."

"You did?" Briana grimaced and wriggled her lips as she struggled not to cry. "My tears were *that* phony? Maybe we need to find somebody else to do this . . ."

"No, no. I didn't mean it like that. I'm sorry, Briana. Don't cry. I think you're a terrific actress and—"

"Psyche!" Briana fluttered her eyes and smiled.

"Dag. You are *good*, girl."

"I know. So, Riley—what do you want to add to Sara's act?"

"Some photographs and video clips."

"You're making her a *video*?"

"Yeah."

"I don't have a video for my song."

"You don't want this one. It'll be full of interviews Sergeant Lorincz will, hopefully, be sending us ASAP. Video clips of the cooks from some of the dining facilities where my father's troops ate the tainted pancakes this year. They'll testify how they fed the guys Protein-Power Pancakes from Mobile Meals Manufacturing."

"And the photographs?"

"Oh, I'm not exactly sure what they'll show. Maybe bulldozers digging up the golf course. Maybe dump trucks loaded down with black garbage bags."

"Maybe? *Maybe?* You don't know?"

"Nope. Not until Jamal and I sneak into the president's office at the country club."

Mongo raised his hand. "Why are you guys going to do that?"

Riley grinned slyly. "So we can grab Mr. Sowicky's camera out of Mr. Paxton's desk."

WAITERS WERE PLACING SILVERWARE, GLASSES, and napkins folded into swan shapes on the cloth-covered tables in the Cranbrook Ballroom as the All-School All-Stars arrived for their final rehearsal.

Riley, Jake, Jamal, and Briana stood on the elevated stage, set up right in front of the ballroom's floor-to-ceiling windows. Mongo was off on a "reconnaissance mission" to make sure the diesel-powered portable floodlight tower was still parked near the construction crew's trailer.

"This is fabtastic!" whispered Briana as she checked out the view of the golf course through the floor-to-ceiling windows behind the stage. "You can totally see the ninth hole!"

"I know," said Riley.

"Hey, Jake?" cried Mr. Holtz from the back of the room. He was carrying a milk crate full of black cables and had a painfully puzzled look on his face. "Got a minute?"

"Sure thing, Mr. Holtz," said Jake.

"These microphone cords are all in a jumble and the mixer board is new and a bunch of these kids are singing to videos and . . . ah, it's a mess."

Riley gave Jake a knowing nod.

"On my way," said Jake, tucking his hands into the front pocket of his hoodie.

"Stick with Jake," Riley said to Jamal. "See what gear they've got that we might be able to use."

"On it," said Jamal. "Yo, Jake. Wait up, bro."

As the two guys headed back to help Mr. Holtz, the lobby doors swung open. Sara, Brooke, and Kaylie— all three of them wearing sunglasses and pink feather boas—swept into the ballroom. An entourage of four adults bustled in behind them.

"We'll do hair and makeup at six," Sara barked over her shoulder.

"Yes, Ms. Paxton," said one of her grown-up flunkies.

Riley checked out a guy in Sara's crew and pegged him to be her accompanist because he was hugging a stack of sheet music against his chest. That meant Sara hadn't totally decided on what she and the Star-Spangled Starlettes were going to sing in the show.

Perfect, thought Riley.

One woman in the entourage sort of walked like a stork. She clapped her hands together briskly and, in a clipped German accent, said, "Time to limber up, girls. We do the flap, ball, change, ja? And five, six, seven, eight . . ."

"Oh, give it a rest, Helga," whined Sara. "The walk from the parking lot wore me out."

Helga had to be the choreographer Mr. Paxton had told them about. The *Broadway* choreographer.

"You ready?" Riley whispered to Briana.

"Ready."

"Briana!" Riley exploded. "Why won't you listen to me?"

"Because you're wrong, Riley! I don't want to go on last."

"Last is best. You'll be the big finish!"

"Yeah—I'll be totally finished if I sing that stupid song you suggested!"

Smiling, Sara wafted ever so gracefully toward the stage as pink feathers fluttered from her fluffy scarf. Her backup singers and entourage trailed behind her.

"Stupid?" Riley fumed. "*Stupid?* You're stupid."

"You're right. I am stupid for ever having listened to

you. Get out of my life, Riley Mack!"

"No. You get out of mine."

"Fine. I will!" Her face burning bright red, Briana stormed out of the ballroom.

Riley stood on the stage shaking his head.

"What's wrong, Riley?" Sara said coyly. "Girl trouble?"

"Ah, Briana thinks I'm stupid for saying she should go on last."

"Oh, *ja*," said the choreographer. "Last is always best. Leave them with the big bang."

"Plus," said Riley, "she won't sing this song!"

He whipped out the sheet music he had downloaded.

"What is it?" asked Sara.

"Only General Joseph C. Clarke's favorite song in the whole world." He handed the paper to Sara. "The general is one of the judges."

"I know that," said Sara, studying the song's lyrics. "'Mix a pancake, stir a pancake, pop it in the pan?'"

"It's a British nursery rhyme from like the eighteen-hundreds."

"So?"

"General Clarke's mother, who was British, used to sing it to him every night before she tucked him in!"

"Really?" Sara sounded skeptical.

"How do you know this?" asked the choreographer.

"Because my dad's in the army! Everybody in the

army knows General Clarke's favorite song."

"It is a classic," gushed the accompanist. "And, well, the choreography simply *leaps* off the page!"

"Ja," said the choreographer, miming someone stirring a pot, then flipping a spatula.

Sara glared at Riley hard. Brooke and Kaylie were right behind her, glowering over her shoulder. "How do we know you're telling the truth, Riley Mack?"

"Look, you guys, it's your call. Jake and I even worked up this awesome video montage for the pancake song. It's way better than the video Briana put together for her stupid *Shrek* number."

Sara's jaw dropped. "Briana has a video?"

"Well, duh. Just about everybody in the competition will be singing to a video!"

"We'll sing 'The Pancake Song,'" said Sara. "And we want your video, too."

"But—"

"You want me to beat Briana, don't you?"

"Yes."

She turned on her heel. "Mr. Holtz?" she shouted. "Please tell Tony Peroni that we will be singing 'The Pancake Song' instead of 'God Bless America.'"

Mr. Holtz looked up from his sound-control board, holding a jumbled tangle of wires. "What?"

Sara stomped her foot. "'The Pancake Song' is ours and we're going on last and Riley Mack's running video for us and if you say no I'm calling home right now and telling my daddy to cancel this whole stupid show and don't think I won't do it either!"

"Fine. Whatever."

Sara, Brooke, and Kaylie—followed by their entire production crew—swept out of the ballroom.

The speakers buzzed to life.

"Test, test, test," said Jake into a cordless microphone, his voice echoing around the room. "We're good to go, Mr. Holtz."

"Let us know if you require further technical assistance," added Jamal.

Then the two of them ambled across the ballroom to join Riley.

"Mr. Holtz asked me to run the sound board tonight," said Jake. "Tony Peroni makes him nervous."

Riley grinned. "Sweet. Our work here is done. Come on, Jamal. We need to go check out Mr. Paxton's office. See if he still has the groundskeeper's camera in his drawers."

"You mean his desk?" said Jamal.

"Yeah."

"Good because I sure don't want to go looking for a camera in that stuck-up old fart's underpants."

RILEY LED JAMAL AND JAKE down the wood-paneled corridors.

"Hang on," said Jake, putting his hand to the Bluetooth listening device in his ear. "It's Mongo."

"What's his status?" asked Riley as he scanned the doorways, looking for a plaque that said MR. PAXTON, PRESIDENT, or CHIEF POISON PEDDLER—something like that.

"The rolling floodlight tower is right where it's supposed to be. The backhoe, too. No sign of Curly and Larry."

"Good," said Riley.

"Since there's no one around, Mongo's going to haul

the floodlight cart closer to the fairway."

"Works for me," said Riley.

"Now he's grunting," reported Jake.

"Huh?" said Jamal.

"Diesel-powered generators with collapsible light towers on top of heavy-duty trailer frames weigh as much as a small truck," said Jake.

Riley nodded. Larry and Curly probably hauled the lights around the golf course with a bulldozer or a team of mules. Riley and his crew had something even stronger: Mongo.

"Here it is, Riley Mack," said Jamal, pointing to a brass sign with COUNTRY CLUB PRESIDENT engraved on it. Jamal's hand immediately went to the doorknob. "Locked."

"Can you get us in?"

"Does bacon sizzle in a skillet?" Jamal crouched down and examined the doorjamb. "No deadbolt." He pulled a plastic card out of his wallet.

"You have a credit card?" said Jake.

"Nah, man. This was our motel room key at Disney World. They said I could keep it as a souvenir."

Jamal slid the key card down the crack between the door and the frame. When it was parallel with the doorknob, he angled it in and pushed until it slid some more.

"Got it."

"Hang on," said Riley. "No sense all of us risking this."

"Risking what?" said Jamal.

"Getting caught breaking and entering."

"Oh. Right. This is illegal."

"Well, what about selling poisoned pancake mix to the army?" asked Jake.

"Oh, that's illegal, too," said Jamal. "Just aren't any cops looking out for it on a daily basis, is all."

"We need to move fast," said Riley. "There could be security cameras back here."

"Not to worry," said Jake. "I've been checking for surveillance equipment ever since we left the ballroom. We're clear."

"Good to know," said Riley. "Okay, Jake—meet us at my house in thirty minutes. If we find any incriminating photographs on Mr. Sowicky's camera, we'll work them into Sara's music video."

"About that video," said Jamal. "How are we gonna pull that off?"

"Easy," said Jake. "Head to YouTube. Search for 'Pancake Song.' Download a couple clips."

"Exactly," said Riley. "See you in thirty minutes."

"Unless, of course, we get busted," said Jamal. "Then, we'll see you in like thirty years, if we get time off for good behavior, which, you know, may not happen, seeing as how everybody keeps calling us 'trouble-makers.'"

Riley arched his eyebrows. "Jamal?"

"Sorry, man," said Jamal. "Nerves."

"Go," Riley said to Jake.

"Right." Jake stuffed his hands into the front pocket of his hoodie and shuffled back up the hallway.

"Let's do it," Riley said to Jamal.

"Doing it," said Jamal, leaning his small shoulder against the door, pushing it open.

They stepped into the office.

Riley eased the door shut. "Check out the top drawer."

"It's locked," said Jamal as he slipped on a sleek pair of black leather gloves and started checking out the various leather cups and penholders on top of Mr. Paxton's desk. "Forgot to pack my lock-picking tools."

"But you brought your gloves?"

"These are my batting gloves. In case we decided to, you know, get up a game today." He rattled the executive desk set's pencil cup. "Score."

"What is it?"

"Paper clip and paper clamp. I'm gonna improvise a lock pick."

While Jamal took apart the clamp and bent the clip,

Riley pressed his ear to the door.

"Anybody coming?" asked Jamal as he worked the straightened paper clip into the small desk lock and used one V from the clamp for sideways torque.

"Yeah. I hear footsteps. Whistling."

"Whistling isn't good," said Jamal, furiously manipulating the tiny levers. "Whistling usually means it's a security guard."

The drawer lock popped open.

"Got it."

Riley moved away from the door, leaned across the desk. "Is there a camera inside?"

"Sure is."

"Power it up. Check out the screen."

Jamal did. Unfortunately, the camera came to life with a jolly "ba-ba-bling!" sound.

"Shhh!" said Riley.

Jamal thumbed some controls. Flipped the camera around so Riley could check the screen.

It was a photograph of a dump truck loaded down with black trash bags.

There was a XYLODYNE DYNAMICS decal on the door.

"Busted!" said Riley.

The door flew open.

Jamal hid the camera behind his back.

Riley spun around.

The whistler *was* a security guard.

"Riley?"

"Um, hi, Sergeant Chambliss."

Fortunately, it was Godfather #24. Chick Chambliss. The former soldier who used to be in his dad's army battalion.

"What're you boys doing back here? This is the club president's office."

"Yeah," said Riley, thinking fast. "Mr. Paxton asked us to grab his camera."

Jamal smiled and held up the digital camera.

Mr. Chambliss's steely-eyed scowl softened. Slightly.

"His daughter's in the talent show," explained Jamal.

"Mr. Paxton wanted us to get some snapshots of the dress rehearsal for him," said Riley.

"Which is just about over," said Jamal.

Mr. Chambliss stepped aside and pointed toward the open door. "Then hustle, men. Hustle!"

Riley shot him a two-finger salute off his eyebrow. "Yes, sir, sir!"

He and Jamal ran down the hall, around the corner, past the ballroom, through the 19th Hole Lounge, across the outdoor dining deck, onto the fairway, and into the woods. In fact, they didn't stop running until they reached the shady spot in a clump of trees where they had hidden their bikes.

Then they pedaled hard and fast, heading for Riley's house.

They had photographs to download and edit into a music video all about pancakes smothered with toxic chemicals instead of butter and syrup!

MORE FOOTAGE FOR THE VIDEO arrived at five p.m. (or one thirty in the morning, Afghanistan time).

"I was able to rouse a couple of the cooks," said Sergeant Lorincz, his grainy image flickering inside the videoconference box on Riley's laptop. "Hauled them out of their bunks. Explained the situation. One guy even took me to his pantry. They still had an unopened sack of Protein-Power Pancake Mix sitting on the shelves."

"Is it from Mobile Meal Manufacturing?"

"Roger that. I zoomed in tight for a close-up on the label. That link working for the footage?"

"Downloading it now, sir," reported Jake from over at

Riley's homework table where he was working laptop number two.

"Good. You'll hear these cooks say they've been serving these Protein-Power Pancakes for more than a year."

"Did you confiscate any powder?"

Sergeant Lorincz grinned. "Roger that, Mr. Mack. I then turned it over to a bomb guy I know who's an expert in all kinds of chemical analysis. I, of course, assumed that was what you would do."

"Outstanding."

"We're good to go on this end," the sergeant continued. "Your father's advocate will have the internet connection up and running at oh-seven-hundred hours."

Riley did the math in his head one more time: with an eight-and-a-half-hour time difference, Larry and Curly had to be digging up the golf course with their backhoe by ten thirty Fairview time so his dad's defenders could show it to the judge (or whatever the military had) as soon as the hearing started.

"Okay, Sergeant," said Riley. "Thanks for going the extra mile for my dad."

"Any of his men would, Riley. Colonel Richard Mack is a rare and remarkable leader."

"Just like his son," said Jamal, leaning in so the laptop camera could capture his smiling face. "Semper Fi, Sergeant. Semper Fi."

Sergeant Lorincz chuckled. "That's the marines' motto, mister."

"I know sir," said Jamal. "It means 'always faithful.' I looked it up."

"We're army, not marines."

"Oh. Let me get back to you on that . . ."

"Okay, Sergeant Lorincz," said Riley. "We gotta go. Tell my dad we won't let him down."

"Will do, Riley. See you at oh-seven-hundred hours."

"Riley?"

Riley whipped around.

His mother was standing in the doorway.

Judging from the horrified look on her face, she'd been standing there for a while.

"Um, well, I gotta go . . ." Riley said to the computer screen. "See you in school on Monday, Sarge."

He slapped down the lid on his laptop.

"Hey, Mom. You're home early."

"Who was that?"

"Oh, this guy from school. Scott Sargensky. We all call him 'Sarge.'"

"What's going on, Riley? Is your father in some kind of trouble? Was that Sergeant Lorincz?"

Riley sighed.

He could not lie to his mother.

Especially not about something this huge.

It was time to add a new member to his crew.

"Yeah, Mom. It's bad. And, we're gonna need your help."

Riley quickly brought his mother up to speed.

He told her everything.

About the dead fish, and the polluted water, and the high levels of nitrogen in the watershed, and how Mr. Paxton was trying to kiss up to the EPA by asking Mr. Kleinman to be a judge at the talent show, and how they had found poisoned pancake powder buried under a sand trap, packages of a mix meant for the military, which was why Mr. Paxton was also kissing up to General Clarke, and how that was why Paxton needed Riley's mom, Mrs. Army Hero Mack, at the talent show. But some of this exact same pancake mix may have made soldiers in Afghanistan sick and now somebody over there was trying to blame Colonel Richard Mack, which is why they had tossed him into the brig, and he had a disciplinary hearing about it first thing tomorrow morning, which would be nine thirty tonight in Fairview.

Next, he told her all about Operation Flapjack and Larry and Curly and the backhoe and the video camera and the linkup with Afghanistan and how great it was that General Clarke and the EPA would be there to verify all the evidence the construction goons dug up.

His mom didn't say a word the whole time Riley monologued.

She just sat there on the edge of his bed, calmly listening, nodding, and waiting until Riley unloaded absolutely everything.

When he finally said, "And that's basically it," she stood up.

Smoothed out her pants.

And exploded.

"Why in blazes didn't you tell me about this sooner?"

"Because, well, Dad and I didn't want to ruin your big night at the country club."

"Riley?"

"Yes, ma'am?"

"The next time something this major is going on? Ruin my night."

"Okay. Good to know."

His mom took a deep breath. "So, is this what you guys do when you hang out together?"

"Only when we have to, Mrs. Mack," said Jamal.

"Well, you've certainly been busy."

"Chya!" said Jamal. "And they call it summer 'vacation'!"

"All right, Riley. What do you need me to do?"

"Well, I was kind of thinking it would be awesome if you could coordinate things inside the ballroom at the judge's table. Make sure none of our heavy hitters leave before they see what we need them to see."

His mom nodded. "And then, when Briana starts screaming at the windows, I need to encourage the general and Mr. Kleinman to run outside and investigate, find out what all the fuss is about."

"Perfect," said Riley. "That'll free me up to head out to the golf course with the remote video cam the instant Mongo blasts the green with the floodlights."

"Works for me," said his mom. "So, do you have a sample of this poison pancake powder?"

"Yeah. In my backpack."

"Can you lend me a cup or two?"

"It's pretty toxic stuff, Mom."

"Don't worry, hon, I'll be careful. I just want to add a little something *extra* to Operation Flapjack."

"What?"

"Oh, let's call it *dessert*."

"Um, most people eat pancakes for breakfast," said Jake.

"But," said Jamal, "I believe your mom plans on making Mr. Paxton his 'just deserts.' Am I right, Mrs. Mack?"

Her grin grew wider. "Exactly."

RILEY AND HIS WHOLE CREW (which now included his mom) arrived at the Brookhaven Country Club about two minutes before the fancy dinner was supposed to start.

Riley's mom parked the van herself—just in case the valet parking attendants got nosy about all the gear being lugged into the country club.

Riley stepped out first, carrying his backpack with the helmet cam stuffed inside. "Communications check," he said.

Mongo, Jake, Briana, and Jamal all crawled out of the van and touched their left ears, where they had each tucked in a miniature Motorola H9 Bluetooth.

"Coming in four by four," said Jamal, turning to Riley's mom, who wasn't wearing her H9 just yet because she wanted to show off the sparkly earrings her husband had given her on her last birthday. "Four by four is military lingo for 'loud and clear,' Mrs. Mack."

"Really?" said Riley's mom, pretending that this was news to her.

"Roger that," said Jamal. "That's military talk, too."

"Okay, you guys," said Briana, tugging a rolling suitcase. "The show starts at nine. I need to head to the ladies' room and change into my fancy dress."

"Are your folks coming to see you perform?" asked Riley's mom.

"Um, no. That would cost like a thousand bucks for two tickets. I figured I'd tell them about the show *after* I win."

"Good idea. And good luck up there, even though, as a judge, I shouldn't say that or let you know that I'm rooting for you!"

"Thanks, Mrs. Mack! Catch you guys later!" Briana dragged her wheelie into the country club.

"Well, we'd better head inside, too," said Mrs. Mack, who was toting a purse plus a small shopping bag. "Dinner starts at seven thirty and I still need to swing by the kitchen. So come on—let's do this thing!"

"I'm with you on that, Mrs. Mack," said Jamal as the gang marched under the country club's grand portico toward the impressive entrance.

A guy wearing a vest and top hat held open a door and they all stepped into a vestibule filled with stuffed chairs and stuffy-looking sofas. The lobby of the Cranbrook Ballroom had been decorated with patriotic streamers, balloons, and bunting.

Mr. Paxton, decked out in a tuxedo, stood waiting patiently for his final judge to arrive. A woman who sort of looked like a mannequin was standing next to him in a sequined gown. Her skinny face was tighter than bicycle pants on a water buffalo. Riley figured it was Mrs. Paxton, Sara's mom.

General Clarke stood beside the Paxtons, his chest a neatly ordered garden of multicolored military ribbons and medals.

Mr. Kleinman, from the EPA, stood next to the general. He was also wearing a tuxedo—one that looked like it had been in storage since his high-school prom back in the 1980s.

"Mrs. Mack!" said Mr. Paxton, putting on his smarmiest smile. "My, you look radiant this evening."

"Nyes," said Mrs. Paxton through pinched lips. "Indeed. Wadiant."

"Thank you," said Riley's mom, demurely showing off the shimmering gown that made her look like a movie star walking the red carpet.

"And I love the eawwings," said Mrs. Paxton. Her lips

were pulled back so tightly, she had trouble pronouncing her *R*s.

"Thank you. Mack gave them to me the last time he was stateside."

"Mack is what everybody calls my dad," Riley piped up. "The guys in his squad."

General Clarke stepped forward. "Mrs. Mack, it is a true honor to finally meet you. When Prescott told me that you were to be one of the judges of this talent competition, well, I immediately signed on for the duty."

"Thank you, General Clarke. That's very sweet of you to say."

"I'm Irving Kleinman, from the Environmental Protection Agency. This is my first judging gig. Gig is a word show people use. If we were giving out an award for Best Dressed, you'd have my vote, Mrs. Mack!"

"Thank you for the compliment," said Riley's mom, "but I believe Mrs. Paxton would be the winner in that category. Is *Mrs.* Kleinman here tonight?"

"Oh, no." He donkey laughed. "I'm single. Still living *la vida loca*!"

"And who, may I ask, are these other children?" asked Mr. Paxton.

"Riley's friends. They're helping out with the show." She turned to Mongo. "Maybe you can find a vending machine or something and grab a quick snack. I think

I have some quarters . . ."

"Nonsense!" said General Clarke. "These young men are eating dinner with us, right, Prescott?"

"Well, the table is only set for—"

"However many we tell them to set it for!"

"Of course, General," said Mr. Paxton. "Please, gentlemen. Join us."

"Thanks!" said Mongo. "I'm starving."

"*Nyes*. I imagine you are."

"What's your name, young man?" the general said to Mongo.

"Hubert Montgomery."

"And these are my friends Jake and Jamal," said Riley.

"Well, it is a pleasure to meet all of you."

Meanwhile, Mr. Paxton was suspiciously eyeing Riley and Jamal's backpacks. He didn't particularly like the looks of Jake's cardboard box crammed full of electronic gear, either.

"Would you gentlemen like to check your bookbags and, er, boxes at the coat-check room?"

Riley hesitated. They needed their gear and gizmos.

"Well, uh . . ."

"Jake's helping Mr. Holtz run the sound for the talent contest," said Riley's mom. "And Riley, Hubert, and Jamal need their backpacks and books. It might be Saturday but these boys know the rules: if they finish dinner early, they need to start their homework."

"But," said Mrs. Paxton, "school's out for the summer."

"I know!" said Riley's mom. "That's why homework is even more important."

"Bravo," said General Clarke. "The world needs more parents like you, Mrs. Mack."

Riley grinned.

He totally agreed.

MR. PAXTON LED THE WAY into the Cranbrook Ball-room.

Riley hung back a few paces with Jake.

"You need help hooking up the computer?"

"Nope."

"What about the receiver for my head cam?"

"We'll link up via a wireless connection. The footage will stream straight into the overseas connection."

"And Sara Paxton's 'Pancake Song' music video?"

"I put it in my cloud and will download it into the show computer as soon I hit the control booth."

Riley draped his arm over his friend's shoulder.

"You're good at this."

"Yeah. I know."

The tables in the ballroom were decorated with red-white-and-blue centerpieces made out of flowers and flags. A control booth—basically a chorus riser crammed with racks of audio and video equipment—was set up near the rear exit. Mr. Paxton pointed to an empty table close to the stage with a RESERVED sign planted on it. "That's our table, ladies and gentlemen."

"Wonderful," said Riley's mom. "We're so close to the stage, we'll be able to see *all* the exciting action!"

"*Nyes,*" said Mr. Paxton, leading the way through the enormous ballroom. "Now then, the speeches and show will start promptly at nine forty-five p.m. This year, there will be seven acts instead of the usual six."

"Oh, right," said Riley's mom. "I heard Tony Peroni asked Briana Bloomfield to be his wild-card pick. Isn't that fantastic?"

"*Nyes.*"

"Is Mr. Peroni here?"

"Not yet."

"He had anothaw wedding to poofoam at," added Mrs. Paxton, her lips barely budging.

"But, he'll be here in plenty of time to emcee the show and, of course, help you folks pick a winner," said Mr. Paxton. "Our last act will most likely go on around ten thirty, ten thirty-five. So, with your voting and a brief award ceremony, we should be done at eleven, eleven fifteen at the latest. Afterward, you're all invited to join me in the Nineteenth Hole Lounge for a champagne reception."

"Whoo-hoo!" said Mr. Kleinman. "Champagne. What I like to call 'giggle juice.'"

Riley figured the EPA guy didn't get out much on Saturday nights unless there was an oil spill or something. Just as everybody sat down, Mr. Holtz, sweating worse than Tony Peroni without a piano player, scurried over to the table.

"Jake? I am so glad you're here early! Some of the wires got disconnected and my hard drive says it's having a fatal error and . . ."

"No problem, Mr. Holtz," said Jake, getting up from his seat and grabbing his cardboard crate. "I even brought some extra cables and junk from home."

"You're a lifesaver!"

"What about your dinner?" asked Riley's mom.

"He can have half of my sandwich," said Mr. Holtz.

"Cool," said Jake as he followed the panicked teacher to the rear of the room. Riley knew Jake would immediately start tinkering with all the wires and cables and inputs they needed to broadcast this evening's action live overseas.

"Um, Riley?"

"Yes, Mongo?"

"I'm starving. So, if Jake isn't . . ."

"Yes. You can have his dinner, too."

"Awesome!"

"Good evening, all."

Uh-oh. Police Chief John Brown was in the house. Dressed in a plaid suit that didn't quite button across his belly, he eyeballed Jamal, Mongo, and, most especially, Riley.

"Good evening, Chief Brown," said Mr. Paxton.

"Are these young men on the judges' panel?"

"They're my dinner dates," said General Clarke.

"Well, my wife and I are sitting right over there," said the chief, jabbing his thumb over his shoulder. "Remember boys, this is a country club, not the school cafeteria. If anyone tries to start a food fight in here . . ."

"We'll help you break it up, sir," said Riley. "Right, Mongo?"

"Definitely." His mouth was crammed full of bread and butter. He'd already found the roll basket.

The sheriff gave Riley a dirty look. Pointed two fingers at his eyes, then swung them around to point at Riley.

"I'm watching you, Mr. Mack."

"Really?" said Riley's mom. "Because he's not in the show. Mr. Paxton's daughter, Sara, however, is."

"*Nyes,*" said Mr. Paxton.

"Well, enjoy your evening, folks." The chief did the two-fingers-to-his-eyes, two-fingers-to-Riley bit again and wobbled away.

As soon as he was gone, Riley's mom stood up. "Will you gentlemen excuse me? I need to go visit the powder room."

"Of course," said General Clarke, popping up from his chair because, Riley figured, it's what officers and gentlemen do whenever a woman stands up.

"It's out those doors and to your right," said Mr. Paxton, also popping up out of his seat.

"Would you like an escort?" asked Mr. Kleinman, the third to spring up from his chair.

"Thank you, Mr. Kleinman, but I'm sure I can find it. I'll be right back. Riley?"

"Yes, Mom?"

"Be sure you boys behave while I'm gone."

"Yes, ma'am."

Riley grinned as his mother sashayed away.

She had draped her purse over the back of her chair but was carrying the tiny shopping bag she'd brought with her from home.

Riley knew that, when his mom exited the ballroom, she wouldn't be heading to the ladies' room.

She'd go straight to the kitchen and tell the chef what

all-American breakfast food the dignitaries at the head table were demanding for dessert.

That's why she was taking the poisoned pancake *powder* with her to the *"powder* room."

RILEY YAWNED.

Dinner—rubbery chicken covered with golden gravy goop, mashed something, wilted green beans, and chocolate mousse (a fancy kind of pudding) for dessert—was over and Mr. Paxton was up at the podium making a pompous speech.

"Welcome to Greens for the Army Green! Tonight, we salute the brave men and women of our military who fight to keep us free so we here might enjoy life, liberty, and the pursuit of happiness—better known as chasing a little white ball around eighteen holes!"

The audience applauded.

"It's almost time for Tony Peroni and the talent

contest, but before Tony takes the stage, I'd like to introduce our three other distinguished judges. First up, General Joseph C. Clarke, my long-time partner at the Pentagon. Just this afternoon, we inked a multiyear deal for Xylodyne to continue providing wholesome, nutritious, home-style meals to our brave soldiers over in Afghanistan."

More applause.

Mr. Paxton smiled and gestured toward the wall of windows behind him. "In fact, we closed the deal with a handshake right out there on the brand-new ninth hole green!"

Now there were hearty chuckles mixed in with the applause.

Riley wasn't just bored. He had work to do. He glanced at his watch: 9:48 p.m.

It was go time.

"Mom?"

She nodded and discreetly slipped her Bluetooth receiver into her ear, then worked her hand into her purse to activate the miniature walkie-talkie that would plug her into Operation Flapjack's command-and-control center, better known as the handy talky concealed in Riley's sport coat.

Riley turned to Mongo, who was clinking his spoon around in a sundae dish, scraping up the last brown smears from his second helping of chocolate mousse.

"You want to take that with you?" he whispered.

"Nah," said Mongo. "I'm done."

"Good. I'm heading backstage."

"That means I'm heading outside."

"Jamal? Hang here."

"Hanging," said Jamal.

Jamal was the designated "swing" player for Operation Flapjack. He would be standing by to do whatever needed doing that nobody had figured out would need to be done.

Riley grabbed his backpack and motioned for Mongo to follow. Crouching so they wouldn't block anybody's view of the stage, they scooted across the ballroom and exited out the side doors.

"See you on the fairway," Riley said to Mongo when they hit the corridor.

"See ya!" Mongo hustled up the hall and out the door. He had floodlights to roll into place.

Riley gave Mongo three minutes to make it around the country club building and over to the construction crew's trailer area.

While he waited, he could hear his mom being introduced. She got more applause than anybody. It was pretty awesome.

At 9:53 p.m., right on schedule, Riley tapped a button on his handy talky. It was time for a radio check.

"Jake?"

"Here."

That made Riley smile. Jake thought this was roll call, like in school.

"All set?"

"Locked and loaded."

"Jamal?"

"Present."

"Mom?"

"Achoo!"

Riley took her sneeze to be her sneaky way of saying, "Here!"

"Mongo?"

Riley heard a lot of heavy breathing.

"Mongo?"

"Okay. Made it. I'm here. Had to run. Ate too much. Mousse."

Now Riley heard an *urp!*

"Okay," said Mongo. "Better."

"Briana?"

"Here."

"I'm coming in. We need to make the backhoe call."

"Hang on. Sara, Brooke, and Kaylie are in here, too. If they see us talking together, they'll know we faked them out with our pretend fight."

"Don't worry. I've got it covered."

Riley headed down the hall to the private banquet room the talent show cast was using as a dressing room.

"Hi, Riley!" It was Sara Paxton. She, Brooke, and Kaylie were all dressed in chef's hats and aprons. "Is the general here?"

"Yep. And, get this—" Riley leaned in dramatically. The three girls clustered around him. "The general told this other judge, Mr. Kleinman, that he hoped someone would be singing 'The Pancake Song' tonight."

Sara gasped. "No. Way."

"And Mr. Kleinman?"

"Yeah, yeah?"

"He said it was *his* favorite song, too!"

The girls put their hands over their mouths, squealed, then bounced up and down like they had to pee real bad.

Riley looked across the room at Briana in her angelic white gown. "Poor Briana. She is going to lose. Big-time."

"So?" said Sara.

"Well, we used to be friends."

"Hah. Everybody *used* to be friends with Briana Bloomfield. We dumped her a year ago."

"I know. But I should at least tell her I'm sorry for blowing up like I did earlier."

"Whatever."

Riley walked across the room.

"Um, Briana?"

"What do you want, traitor?"

"Can I talk to you? Outside?"

Briana huffed an exasperated sigh. "I guess."

The two of them hurried out the door.

"What'd you tell the three wicked witches?"

"Exactly what they wanted to hear." Riley dug a cell phone out of his sport jacket. It had the pitch modulator attached to it.

"I'm Mr. Paxton again, right?"

"Right. Jake rigged this thing so Curly's caller ID window will read 'Xylodyne Dynamics' when we're connected."

"Fabtastic."

Riley handed Briana the phone.

"It's ringing!"

Riley leaned in, tight against Briana's ear, so he could hear both sides of the conversation.

"That you, Mr. Paxton?" snapped Curly the instant he picked up the call.

"Nyes," said Briana. "I need you fellows to start digging up the gold immediately. The talent show is about to commence and . . ."

"Forget it, pal."

"I beg your pardon?"

"I said forget it. We ain't diggin' up nothin'. Youse can have it all."

"I'm sorry, I don't understand . . ."

"Then, let me paint you a picture: Larry and me are currently situated on a white, sandy beach far, far away from Fairview. A secluded-type place where you can't never find us."

"But what about our agreement?"

"Agreement, schmeement. Once we dug up your gold for youse, you'd send some of your navy SEAL and army commando buddies over to dig *us* an early grave. We ain't dumb, Mr. Paxton. We play video games. We know how these things work."

"But, I assure you . . ."

"Enjoy your buried treasure, Mr. Paxton. The gold is all yours."

The line went dead.

So did Riley's dreams of rescuing his father.

46

RILEY LOOKED AT BRIANA.

Briana looked at Riley.

"They're gone?" she said. "Curly and Larry? We've lost our two guys with the backhoe?"

Riley nodded.

"Now what do we do? Riley?"

Riley glanced at his cell phone.

It was 10:06 p.m. They had less than thirty minutes before his father's hearing started.

He was about to strike out for the third time in less than a month!

"Aren't those Rockin' Rollers amazing?" he heard

Tony Peroni's voice boom over the loudspeaker in the ballroom.

The talent show had started.

"Beautiful. I mean that, kids. Sincerely. Our next act comes from Crestwood Middle School, and wait till you see what this kid can do with a rubber duck!"

When Riley linked up with Afghanistan, he definitely needed to show his dad (not to mention everybody else in the room) a live video feed of something much more interesting than some kid squeaking out "Jingle Bells" on a tub toy or Sara Paxton singing "The Pancake Song"!

They needed a new plan. Operation Flapjack was a flop.

"Riley?" said Briana. *What are we gonna do?*

Suddenly, the answer hit him.

"We're gonna do what we do best. Improvise."

"Oh-kay. And how, exactly, are we going to do that?"

"I'm not sure. I need to go see what I can dig up. In the meantime—stall!"

"There's only three more acts after the squeaky ducky, then I go on, then Sara."

Riley nodded. He thumbed the talk button on the handy talky in his coat pocket. "Okay, everybody. We're going to plan B."

"Achoo-bee?"

Yes, his mom had apparently decided to use nothing

286

but sneezes to communicate.

"I'm not sure, Mom. Stand by for updates. Mongo?"

"Yeah?"

"You all set up?"

"Yeah. But, Riley, the lights are off in the construction trailer. I don't think those guys with the backhoe are here yet."

"I know."

His mom sneezed again. This time, it sounded like a sloppy, "Wha-a-at?"

"It's a long story. Mongo, meet me at the trailer. We need to find some kind of hand tools. A shovel. A hoe."

"Okay. I already found a bucket of golf balls."

"Wait," whispered Jake, "the poisoned pancake powder is buried *six feet deep.*"

"I'll dig fast," said Riley. "Mongo can help."

"Sure I can," said Mongo.

"You only have like twenty-some minutes, Riley," said Jake.

"You need the backhoe, man," whispered Jamal.

"I know. Do you know how to hotwire one?"

"Sorry. I do locks and magic tricks, not motor vehicles."

"I-doo," sneezed his mom.

"Mom?"

"Ah, ah—diesel?" It was amazing how many different sneezes she could come up with.

"I guess," said Riley. "I know it's a John Deere."

"Screwdriver!" This she said out loud.

Riley could hear a passing waiter in the distance say, "Right away, ma'am."

"I thought most people drank screwdrivers for breakfast." Now smarmy Mr. Kleinman was whispering to Riley's mom.

"Oh, they're good anytime," his mom whispered back. "Especially if you need to get your motor running."

"I found a screwdriver in a toolbox," reported Mongo.

"Great. Meet me at the backhoe. Mom? Stand by to walk me through it!"

RILEY GRABBED HIS BACKPACK, RACED up the hallway, slammed through the exit door, flew around the front of the country club, hopped a hedge, dodged a couple of trees, and found Mongo standing next to the big yellow backhoe proudly holding a giant screwdriver.

They had fifteen minutes to pull this off.

"Okay, Mom. I'm here."

"Oops," his mom said. "I dropped my napkin. Okay, Ri. I'm back under the table."

"Cool."

"Not really. We have a situation."

"Now what?"

"The tap dancer who was supposed to go on before

Briana got so nervous, he threw up. Briana is on *now*."

Riley heard beautiful singing in the background.

"She's good, isn't she?"

"Fantastic. But, Riley? Even if Briana does an encore, you won't have enough time to get out to the ninth hole and dig up the buried treasure before Sara goes on. We may lose our audience, not to mention our official witnesses!"

Riley scrunched up his face. Thought hard.

"You okay, Riley?" asked Mongo.

"Yeah."

"'Cause your face is all scrunched up. . . ."

"Jamal?"

"Yo?"

"You got your magic tricks in your backpack?"

"Never leave home without them."

"Okay. If Briana has to leave the stage before we're ready for the big reveal, you jump up and start doing your act. Say you're the upchucker's best friend and you demand the chance to go on in his place."

"All right," said Jamal. "The swing is swinging into action."

"Mom?"

"Yes?"

"You back Jamal up. Be real mom-ish."

"Mom-ish?"

"You know what I mean." Riley pitched his voice up

into a falsetto: "*'Give the boy a chance. It's only fair.'*"

There was a silence. For like two seconds.

"Is that what I sound like?"

"Not usually." Riley grabbed the screwdriver from Mongo, climbed up into the backhoe, and crawled underneath the dashboard. "Okay. I'm under the ignition. I see two wires anchored to two screw posts."

"Hold on to the screwdriver's plastic handle and lay the metal shaft across the two connectors. It should start right up."

"How do you know this stuff, Mom?"

"I dated your father. In Indiana."

"Hang on. I'm gonna give it a try."

"Hurry!"

Riley maneuvered the screwdriver into place.

He saw a couple sparks but nothing happened.

"Mom? It's not working."

"Try again."

Riley did.

"Nothing."

"You're sure you're making contact with both connectors?"

"Yes!"

"Mrs. Mack?"

A new voice under the table: Mr. Paxton.

"Is everything all right?"

"Yes. Now. I was just feeling a little dizzy. Needed to

put my head between my knees."

"I see. Well, as a judge, you really should watch the show . . ."

"Okay. I'm feeling better. Here I come. Sorry."

Riley knew that "Sorry" was for him.

He slammed the screwdriver handle down hard on the metal floor.

"Are you okay, Riley?" asked Mongo.

"No. I'm terrible."

And then things got even worse.

A blinding flashlight snapped on.

Riley could barely make out the shadow of a man behind the beam.

"What're you doing down there, little dude?"

IT WAS MR. SOWICKY!

The golf course's former head groundskeeper. The guy Riley and his crew more or less got fired.

"You want me to take care of this guy?" asked Mongo, working his hands into fists.

Riley shook his head. "No." He turned to Mr. Sowicky. "We found your camera. You were right. Mr. Paxton was burying something extremely toxic underneath the golf course."

"I knew it, man."

"We want to dig it up and show everybody. Tonight. While the EPA guy and the Pentagon general are here."

"I know. Briana told me."

"What?"

"I live like two minutes away. Bree texted me. Said you dudes needed help with a backhoe, but she couldn't lay down the details because she had to go onstage and sing 'Hallelujah.'"

"Mr. Sowicky, we need to hurry. We have maybe ten minutes to tear up the ninth hole green."

"How come? Because it's like brand-new and all."

"That's where Mr. Paxton had the landscapers bury all sorts of toxic chemicals and crap! So, can you help us?"

"Fer sure. Only, you can't hotwire this particular John Deere because it has what they call an electric fuel shutoff."

"What's it do?" asked Mongo.

"Shuts off the fuel," said Mr. Sowicky. "Electrically."

"So what can we do to override the shutoff?" asked Riley.

Mr. Sowicky reached into his pocket. "Use my key. Larry and Curly asked me to hold on to their spare in case they, you know, ever dropped theirs down a sewer grate or whatever."

Riley finally smiled. "Far out!"

Riley moved out of the way as Mr. Sowicky grabbed hold of a handrail and hauled himself up into the cab. He plopped down into the crinkled leather seat and slipped his key into the ignition. One twist, and the yellow earthmover rumbled to life. Fortunately, the applause and cheering in the ballroom was so loud, nobody heard the backhoe start up.

Unfortunately, that meant Briana had finished singing. Early.

"So, do you actually know how to operate a backhoe, Mr. Mack?"

"No. Not really."

"Well, scrunch in there. It's time for your first lesson."

"Yes, sir!" Riley squeezed in behind the driver's seat. "Mongo?"

"Yeah?"

"Toss me my backpack. I need the helmet cam."

"You got it."

Mongo heaved Riley's JanSport up into the cab.

"Thanks. Stand by to hit the spotlights!"

"Good luck, guys!" Mongo took off through the trees and lumbered as fast as he could to the fairway.

Riley punched the talk button on his handy talky.

"Okay, everybody, we're back in business and ready to rumble."

"Ya-hooo," sneezed his mom. Then Riley heard her say, "Come on, let Jamal do his magic act! We're one contestant short. We have time. Then Sara can do her big finish."

"You ready to roll, Mr. Mack?" asked Mr. Sowicky.

"Hang on. One second. I need to make sure we have cover inside the ballroom before we cruise across the fairway."

Mr. Sowicky nodded knowingly. "I can dig it. Taking on the Man is never easy, little dude."

"Yeah. Tell me about it."

In his earpiece, Riley heard his mother say, "Jamal *has* to go on. It's what my husband, Colonel Richard Mack, would want."

"You heard Mrs. Mack!" boomed General Clarke. "Let the young man go on!"

"But—" Mr. Paxton started to protest.

Mrs. Paxton jumped in to help him out. "This young man's 'magic' act has not been pwopewee appwoved by ouw appwovoes committee."

"Who cares?" barked the gruff general. "He's a kid. He's an American. He deserves his shot!"

"Fine!" said Mr. Paxton. "You have five minutes, young man."

"Five minutes?" said Jamal. "You hear that, Fluffy? We need to *hop* to it."

Riley heard the audience roar with laughter.

"What'd he do?" Riley asked.

From the control booth, Jake gave him a quick report. "Jamal just pulled a windup bunny rabbit out of his backpack and sent it up the center aisle."

"Outstanding," said Riley. "You ready to connect with Afghanistan?"

"Just give me the word and we'll initiate the uplink."

"Okay, Mr. Sowicky," said Riley as more applause and laughter rocked the ballroom. "Let's do it!"

Mr. Sowicky punched a couple of buttons on a control panel. "Hang on to something, little dude."

The boxy backhoe lurched across the patch of gravel and dirt and crawled down a double-rutted access road to the fairway.

Dead ahead in the distance, Riley could see the humpbacked silhouette of the ninth hole. To his left, maybe a hundred yards away, he could also see the brightly lit windows of the Cranbrook Ballroom and the small, shadowy figure of Jamal sweeping across the stage.

Riley grinned.

It was time for *him* to do a little magic and pull some pancake powder out of the ground.

PRESCOTT PAXTON SAT WATCHING THE young African American boy do a card trick.

With General Clarke.

"Now, show the audience your card, but don't let me see it, sir."

Paxton's face was hurting from pretending to smile.

How much longer would this chatty little fellow prattle on? So far, Jamal the Magnificent, as he called himself, had pulled a rabbit out of his backpack, flowers out of Mrs. Mack's ears, and a bucket of gold coins out of his wife, Mrs. Paxton's, nose.

But he'd be a good sport.

After all, the Pentagon's chief procurement officer

for Near East operations was enjoying the young man's antics and that's what this whole Greens for the Army Green event was really all about: a chance to hobnob with the military brass and bamboozle General Clarke into thinking he and Xylodyne Dynamics actually gave two hoots about the soldiers who consumed their products.

"Now put your card back into the deck, sir . . ."

The least Prescott Paxton could do was suffer through the final tedious moments of this interminable talent show.

His wife leaned in close and whispered in his ear: "Do something, Pwescott! That young wascal is a stage hog."

"*Nyes*, dear . . ."

"*Now*, Pwescott, befowe it's too wate. If that boy keeps chawming Genewa Cwawke wike this, Sawa might wose!"

"Nonsense, dear. Sara is far too talented to lose."

"Pwescott? Do you want to be the one deawing with youw daughtew's mewtdown when this twickstew steaws hew twophy?"

Paxton dabbed his lips with his napkin and thought about the last time Sara hadn't gotten what she wanted. They had to repaint the living room after *that* little tantrum.

He needed to give this young magician the hook, pull

him off the stage. Unfortunately, he couldn't interrupt the card trick being played out with the general.

The boy made quite a production out of pulling a single card from the deck.

"Was this your card, sir? The nine of clubs?"

"Yes!" said General Clarke. "Amazing!"

"Do you like that card, sir? Is the nine of clubs your favorite card in the whole deck?"

"Yes." The general played along.

"Then, presto-change-o, sir!" The boy tapped the squared-off cards and thumb-flicked through the entire deck to show the general and the audience that every single card had magically turned into the nine of clubs.

The audience applauded.

Mr. Paxton saw his chance.

He sprang to his feet and clapped louder than anyone in the room.

"Bravo! Well done!" He pivoted to face the back of the room. "Tony? Will you kindly introduce our final act?"

"I'm not finished," protested the boy on the stage. "For my next trick . . ."

For whatever reason, the boy stopped talking and touched his ear, as if he had just received an incoming call on an invisible cell phone headset.

"Oh, okay," the magician mumbled. Tucking his deck

of cards into his coat pocket, he beamed at the audience and said, "Ladies and gentlemen, for my next trick, I'm gonna disappear."

Tony Peroni strode onstage, laughing and clapping.

"Beautiful, Jamal. I love your act, love your spunk. It's a lovefest in Tony Town. Okay, it's time for our big finish! Time to bring on the act we've all been waiting to see: Sara Paxton and her Star-Spangled Starlettes singing . . ."

Peroni stared at an index card.

Looked off into the wings.

"Is this right?" he mumbled.

"Yes!" whispered Sara from the wings.

"Okay. Here it comes, folks: 'The Pancake Song'!"

The what? thought Paxton. The last time he and his daughter had chatted, she told him she would be singing "God Bless America," one of General Clarke's all-time favorites.

"About time," Sara muttered as she and her two friends bounded onstage, dressed up in floppy hats and aprons like that Italian fellow, Chef Boyardee.

Mr. Paxton stood up to ask his daughter just what she thought she was doing. But as Sara grabbed the microphone and said, "Hit it, maestro!" he saw something even more disturbing.

Through the floor-to-ceiling windows behind the stage. The silhouette of what appeared to be a backhoe lumbering its way across the top of the newly sodded green for the ninth hole.

"What the blazes—" He tossed his napkin down on his seat. "Excuse me, everybody. I have a course-maintenance issue to contend with."

The judges weren't paying attention to him.

They were too busy gawking at the stage in disbelief at the three girls bouncing up and down while making kindergarten hand gestures and singing:

"Mix a pancake,
Stir a pancake,
Pop it in the pan.
Fry the pancake,
Toss the pancake,
Catch it if you can."

As soon as the girls finished the first verse, video screens on both sides of the stage lit up with ridiculous footage of flipping, flopping pancakes.

"Second verse," sang Sara, *"same as the first."*

When they started doing their childish "mixing" and "stirring" choreography for the second time, Mr. Paxton was at Chief Brown's table, whispering in the police officer's ear.

"We have a vandalism situation," said Paxton.

"Where?"

"Outside. On the ninth hole!"

"What's going on?"

Mr. Paxton looked out the ballroom windows again. He almost had a heart attack.

"Some hooligan has commandeered a backhoe and is attempting to dig up one of our brand-new sand traps!"

RILEY AND MR. SOWICKY HAD leveled off the backhoe's outriggers and swiveled around to the rear of the machine.

Riley switched on his helmet cam.

"You getting this, Jake?"

"You're coming in loud and clear. Sara and her pancake flippers are onstage. You want me to run the video clips from the army cooks?"

"Not yet. Wait until we hit the first stack of pancake powder sacks."

"Hey, Riley?" It was Jamal. "I killed big, man. I slayed 'em."

"Great. We're gonna start digging. Mr. Sowicky?"

"All right, little dude, let's rock and roll." He manipulated two knob-topped control levers. "Nothing to it. We boom down, stick out, roll the bucket."

The hydraulics on the toothed shovel stretched the boom out across the sand trap.

"Now we pull the stick in while booming up."

The bucket bit into the sand and scraped a two-foot-deep trench into the ground.

"Swing the boom to the side, roll the bucket, and dump your load."

A pile of sand fell on the fairway.

"Now we just repeat it all again." Mr. Sowicky sent the shovel back to the trench in the sand trap.

"Um, Riley, uh . . ." It was Jake.

"What's up?"

"Mr. Paxton. Chief Brown."

"What about 'em?"

"Mr. Paxton is like pointing at the window and the police chief is flipping open his sport jacket because . . . uh-oh."

"Uh-oh what, Jake?"

"He has a pistol holstered to his belt. They're leaving the ballroom, Riley. They see you!"

"What? Mongo hasn't even switched on the spotlights."

"It's the moon," said Jake. "We forgot to check the moon phase."

Riley glanced up at the night sky.

Yep. There it was. A full June moon. The kind they sing about in love songs.

"Okay, Mr. Sowicky," said Riley, "thanks for the lesson. I'll take it from here."

"What?"

"Trouble's coming. If they catch you doing this, they'll think you're vandalizing the golf course because Mr. Paxton fired you."

"So?"

"Mr. Sowicky, you could go to jail."

"So could you."

"Nah. I'm a kid. The worst that happens to me is I spend the summer at some kind of juvenile delinquent work camp."

"But . . ."

"I've never been to camp. Might be fun. Go. Hurry."

"You sure you know how to . . ."

"Yes."

Mr. Sowicky climbed out of the operator's seat and jumped down from the backhoe.

"Little dude?"

"Yeah?"

"When operating a backhoe, always remember: safety first!"

Riley shot him a two-finger salute. "Gotcha. Thanks."

As Mr. Sowicky ran for the forest, Riley worked the

two levers back and forth. "Okay," he said. "Just like the claw game at the video arcade."

After a few bumps and boom stutters, he swung the bucket back into place and sank it down with a thud.

"My bad," he mumbled as he worked the levers to lower the shovel into the trench and drag it back toward the rig.

When his load was full, he heard a voice shout from maybe a hundred yards away, "What the blazes do you think you're doing?"

It was Mr. Paxton.

"Cease . . . and . . . desist!" cried Chief Brown. He had to catch his breath between words because he wasn't used to running.

Riley dumped his load and swiveled the boom arm back for a third dig.

"Riley?" It was Mongo.

He kept working the lever, kept digging. "Yeah?"

"Mr. Paxton and Chief Brown just ran past me."

"I know . . ."

"The chief has a pistol!"

"Do you still have that bucket of balls?"

"Huh?"

Riley pulled back on the levers, scooped up another load. He could see the tops of the black garbage bags.

"Use them! Chuck a couple golf balls at the chief. Then run like you've never run before!"

"Gotcha!"

Floodlights thumped on. Riley and his backhoe were suddenly bathed in brightness.

"Owww!" he heard chief Brown scream. "That hurt!"

Yeah. Mongo had a wicked sidearm.

"Come back here, you! Freeze! Stop running! This is the police! You can't get away!"

Uh, yeah, Riley thought, *he can.*

The chief was slow. Mongo had his getaway golf cart.

"Jake? Roll the video! Now!"

Riley kept scooping. He hoped the chief wasn't mad and dumb enough to start shooting at a kid who had popped him in the butt with a golf ball. Riley's heart was racing and it didn't stop pounding until he heard Mongo say, "I'm clear. The chief slipped on the fairway when the sprinklers came on all of a sudden."

Riley grinned. *Mr. Sowicky did that!* he thought. *He didn't run away. He ran to the sprinkler control panel!*

"Good luck, you guys," said Mongo. "I'm heading home through the hedges. Say hey to your dad, Riley. Mongo out."

Riley finished his final cut across the trench. The claw edge of the bucket tore open the sides of a few plastic trash bags.

He could see the pancake powder packages.

"Jake?"

"Yeah?"

"I'm going in for the close-up."

Riley swung the boom to the side and jumped out of the backhoe cab. He tumbled sideways when he hit sand. Hauling himself up, he felt for his helmet cam to make sure the lens hadn't been knocked out of alignment.

When he was absolutely certain it was still pointing dead ahead, he turned to the trench he had just dug.

Mr. Paxton was standing inside the six-foot deep hole.

Glaring up at him.

"Hello, Mr. Mack," he said as an extremely creepy smile slithered across his lips. "Too bad your father, the 'war hero,' isn't here to protect you."

And that's when Mr. Paxton pulled out *his* pistol.

MR. PAXTON WAGGLED HIS WEAPON.

"You like it? It's a top-of-the-line Xylodyne semiautomatic G15."

"You sell those to the army, too?"

"Indeed we do. What's that thing on your head? It's not some kind of video camera, is it?"

"This? Nah. It's just a stupid coal miner's lamp that doesn't work. I needed it to see what I was doing when I hot-wired the backhoe."

"Is that so?" said Mr. Paxton, aiming the pistol up out of the trench with a shaky hand while swiping at the sandy dirt in the bottom of the hole with his foot.

He was trying to cover up the sacks the backhoe had just exposed.

"Yeah," said Riley. "I needed a big steam shovel to pay you people back big-time!"

Mr. Paxton cocked his head sideways. "Pay me back? For what?"

Riley pretended to pout. "Not you. Your daughter. I wanted to be in her act, but she wouldn't let me! Said it was 'girls only.' That's not fair, Mr. Paxton. I can sing! I can dance, too!"

Riley broke into what he hoped looked like somebody dancing.

Mr. Paxton lowered his pistol. Smiled devilishly. "That's what this is all about?"

"Well, yeah! Why else would I tear up your stupid golf course? I wanted to pay you back for what your daughter did to me! She crushed my dream, Mr. Paxton. She crushed my dream."

"I see . . ." said Mr. Paxton, reaching up to place his pistol in the sand trap so he could bend down and use both his hands to claw and scrape at the loose dirt at the bottom of the pit. He was trying to cover up the evidence he now thought Riley knew nothing about. "You weren't searching for any kind of, oh, I don't know—buried treasure?"

"Underneath a golf course?" Riley gave that a lip

fart. "Yeah. Right. I'm that dumb. Dig up a golf course to find where the pirates hid their gold after playing eighteen holes. How stupid do you think I am?"

"Incredibly," said Mr. Paxton with a sneer. "To think you could pull off a stunt this blatant and brazen . . ."

Police Chief Brown huffed over the top of the green. His plaid suit was soaking wet. "What's going on back here?"

"I have apprehended our vandal," Mr. Paxton said smugly from down in the scooped-out pit. "Young Riley Mack."

"Well, well, well," said the chief, looping his thumbs under his belt and waddling down the embankment from the green. "Fairview's number-one known troublemaker. What'd you do this time, you redheaded rascal?"

"Nothing!" He gestured toward the pistol lying on the ground. "Can I have my gun back now?"

"Oh," said the police chief, strolling over to confiscate the weapon. "This is yours?"

"Well, it certainly isn't *mine*." Mr. Paxton could lie faster than anyone Riley had ever met.

The chief pocketed the pistol. "My, my, my. Stealing a backhoe? Carrying a concealed weapon?"

"It wasn't concealed!" said Riley, trying to buy as much time as he could. "It was sitting right there, out in the open."

"Tell it to the judge," sneered the chief. "You just earned yourself another free ride in the back of my patrol car. And this time we're going to lock you up and throw away the key."

Riley sniffled. "I want my mommy."

"Ha!" said Chief Brown. "Too bad."

"I want my mommy! Now!"

Riley hoped his mom heard her cue.

"What the heck is that thing on your head?" asked Chief Brown.

"A miner's lamp," said Mr. Paxton.

"The heck it is. There's no lightbulb. Just a lens."

Thinking fast, Riley leaped into the six-foot-deep hole with Mr. Paxton. When he found his footing, he tilted his head down so people in Afghanistan could see the evidence.

"Hey, what's in those plastic trash bags, Mr. Paxton?"

Riley dropped to his knees and started clearing away the thin layer of dirt Mr. Paxton had been pushing around with his shoe.

"Stop that!" shouted Mr. Paxton as he tried to shove Riley to the side.

"Is that pancake powder?" cried Riley as he ripped a ten-pound sack out of the ground.

He held it out at arm's length so his army audience could read the label.

"Protein-Power Pancake Mix?" He flipped the bag

around. "Made by Mobile Meal Manufacturing. Say, isn't that a Xylodyne company, Mr. Paxton?"

Chief Brown stood frozen at the lip of the ditch, looking down and scratching his head. "Why would anybody bury pancake mix under a sand trap?"

"I'll tell you why," said General Clarke as, finally, he, Mr. Kleinman, and Riley's mom made it to the hole. "It's poison!"

"POISON?" MR. PAXTON LAUGHED, PUTTING his hands on his hips, trying to look tough.

But it's extremely hard to look tough when you're standing in a six-foot-deep hole, looking up at people.

"General, please. Don't be absurd."

"We just saw a video clip from some mess hall cooks over in Afghanistan."

Mr. Paxton shook his head like he was trying to unclog his ears. "What?"

"Your daughter sang to a very fascinating music video," said Riley's mom.

"I'll say," added Mr. Kleinman. "It was almost like people were testifying against Xylodyne Dynamics."

"Let me see that sack, son," said General Clarke, settling into a crouch at the edge of the trench.

Riley tossed the bag up out of the hole. The general caught it.

"Yep. This is the same stuff. It's been making our fighting men and women sick." He handed the evidence over to the EPA man. "Can you check this out, Kleinman? Run a few tests?"

"It would be my pleasure, General."

"Hey, look," said Riley, pointing down at the bottom of the ditch. "There's a ton more of that stuff buried right underneath where Mr. Paxton is standing. If it's poison, I wonder if it's what killed all those fish in the water hazard."

"Of course!" said Mr. Kleinman. "The excess nitrogen would seep out and pollute the watershed! Good environmental detective work, son."

"He's very good at science," said Riley's mom. "When he applies himself."

"Keep it up, young man," said Mr. Kleinman. "The EPA could use more minds like yours."

"So could the army," added the general.

"Wait a minute!" shouted Mr. Paxton. "Help me out of this hole, somebody!"

Chief Brown finally shot out an arm and hauled Mr. Paxton out of the trench. The general and his mom helped Riley climb up and out, too.

Mr. Paxton swiped at his dusty tuxedo in an attempt to spruce it up. "This is preposterous! Before you gentlemen jump to any conclusions based on a known troublemaker's slanderous accusations . . ."

Just then, a golf cart came bounding across the fairway.

Jamal was at the wheel. Briana was riding in the passenger seat, balancing something in her lap.

Riley smiled when the cart skidded to a stop because he could see what Briana was holding: a plate stacked high with fluffy pancakes.

"Here you are, Mr. Paxton," said Briana.

"What on earth are those?"

"Protein-Power Pancakes," said Jamal. "We asked the country club chef to whip you up a batch."

"We told him they were your favorite," added Briana.

"And to make sure he used the right pancake mix," said Jamal, "we asked him to take photographs, every step of the way."

He pulled a digital camera out of his pocket.

"Chief Brown?" said Mr. Paxton. "Do something?"

The chief held up both his hands. "I believe this is a military and/or EPA matter now. In either case, it's out of my jurisdiction."

"Can I see that, Jamal?" asked Riley.

"Sure." Jamal tossed the camera over to Riley.

"Wow. Here's some pictures of late-night landscaping

crews burying black plastic trash bags under this very same green. . . ."

"We saw those already," said Mr. Kleinman.

"They were also in your daughter's music video," added the general.

"Chief Brown?" pleaded Mr. Paxton.

The chief threw up his hands again. "Out of my jurisdiction."

"Here we go," said Riley, holding the camera's display so Mr. Paxton could see it. "There's the bag of Protein-Power Pancake Mix we dug up back here a couple days ago. Here's the chef putting the powder in a bowl. Adding water. Whisking it all up. Ladling the batter onto the griddle."

Riley's mom hummed a snatch from "The Pancake Song" while Riley described the photos.

"Yep. He made them just like they make 'em in the mess hall."

"So?" said Mr. Paxton. "There is nothing wrong with Protein-Power Pancakes."

"Is that why you issued that product recall?" asked General Clarke.

"No, sir. The powder shipped overseas simply reached its expiration date earlier than anticipated."

"*Two years* earlier?" said the general.

"Yes. It's hot over in Afghanistan. The mix broke down faster than projected."

"So there's absolutely nothing wrong with these pancakes?" asked Riley.

"Of course not. And I'll prove it in court when I sue you for slandering the good name of Xylodyne Dynamics!"

Riley shrugged. "Okay. If you say so." He pulled the handy talky out of his sport jacket. "Jake?"

"Yeah?"

"You there with Sara?"

"Yeah. In the dressing room. She's kind of hungry. Seems she skipped dinner before the show, on account of her nerves."

"I can relate," said Briana.

"But singing about pancakes has made her super-hungry for some."

"Well, tell her to dig in. Her daddy says there's absolutely nothing wrong with Protein-Power Pancakes."

"See? I told you!" said a voice that sounded an awful lot like Sara Paxton. "Thanks, Daddy! I'm so totally craving pancakes right now!"

"Wait!" shouted Mr. Paxton.

"Yes?" said Riley.

"You made her pancakes from the same mix?"

"Well, duh. You think the chef had time to whip up two different kinds of pancakes and still pull off a fancy banquet?"

"Give me that darn thing!" Paxton grabbed the radio

out of Riley's hand. "Sara? This is your father. Do not eat those pancakes. Do you hear me? Do not even touch them! They could kill you! They're full of chemicals that will make you sick!"

Riley looked over to his mom.

She was smiling. "You think they heard that all the way over in Afghanistan?"

"Definitely," said Riley. "In fact, I believe it went through 'four-by-four.'"

EPILOGUE

MR. PAXTON WAS SURPRISED TO learn, a few minutes later, that his daughter Sara had actually stormed off the stage the instant people started paying more attention to the video screens than her singing.

"Take me home, Mommy!" she had demanded. "This instant!"

Mrs. Paxton had agreed.

That voice on the handy talky?

Pure, prerecorded Briana.

By 11:00 p.m. Eastern Daylight Savings Time, 7:30 a.m. in Afghanistan, Riley's father was totally exonerated.

The board of inquiry, although initially startled by

the "unorthodox methods used for the presentation of evidence in this matter," promptly apologized and promised Colonel Richard Mack that they would get to "the bottom of this matter."

General Clarke made a quick phone call to the Pentagon and initiated the paperwork that would terminate "any and all" contracts between Xylodyne Dynamics and the U.S. military "effective immediately."

"Call your lawyers and insurance companies, Prescott," the general said to Mr. Paxton in the country club parking lot while they waited for the valet parking attendants to bring their cars around. "Your company will be paying for all the medical expenses of each and every one of those soldiers your product so grievously wounded."

"B-b-but, Jack," Mr. Paxton stammered.

"You're right. Why am I bothering to talk to you about this? You won't be CEO of Xylodyne after the market opens on Monday. Not after Wall Street learns what you and your company have done and sends your stock price tumbling down the toilet!"

Mr. Kleinman rushed off to his EPA lab to analyze the pancake powder, even though Riley suggested he could save himself some time and trouble by calling Ms. Kaminski's boyfriend, who had already done the test and confirmed the presence of melamine and cyanuric acid.

After Mr. Kleinman left in his government-issue sedan, Riley's mom and Tony Peroni were the only judges still available to award the first-place trophy to the winner of the talent show.

"We're giving it to songbird Briana Bloomfield," the wedding singer announced. "The Rockin' Rollers come in second, and Jamal the Magnificent, third. Both of those acts will be receiving a fabulous consolation prize: a complete collection of my greatest hits."

"Wow," Jamal whispered to Briana. "That's even sweeter than your ten-thousand-dollar scholarship!"

Before they left the country club, Riley heard a man say to a group gathered in the 19th Hole Lounge, "We need Stuart Sowicky back on the job, first thing tomorrow! He can dig up the rest of whatever that nincompoop Paxton buried under the fairways and give us back our 'green' greens!"

A lot of people in tuxedos and evening gowns said, "Hear, hear!" to that, so Riley felt pretty confident that Mr. Sowicky would be officially *un*fired first thing Sunday morning.

When Riley and his mom finally got home, they linked up once again with Afghanistan for a family chat with Riley's dad (who, in under an hour, had already ID'd the local Xylodyne Dynamics contractor, a guy named

Crumpler, who had started spreading the false rumors against him as part of the Protein-Power cover-up).

"You two did an awesome job," he said proudly.

"Thank you, hon," said Riley's mom.

"So how come you guys were hot-wiring backhoes in Indiana?" asked Riley.

"They were tractors," said his dad. "And, I'm sorry, Riley—you do not yet have clearance for that information."

"And you probably never will," added his mom. Then she leaned in closer to the computer. "Mack, I know there was a lot going on tonight, but did you happen to notice my earrings?"

Riley's dad grinned. "Roger that, Mrs. Mack. They looked almost as amazingly beautiful as you did in that dress."

Riley rolled his eyes while his mom and dad said a bunch more mushy junk. (This was why he and his mom usually had separate chats with his dad: Riley preferred operating in a no-cooties zone.)

Finally, the conversation turned to Riley and his upcoming vacation.

"So," said his dad, "now that school's out, what else do you guys have planned for the summer?"

"Hard to say, Dad. It's kind of like pancake powder under a putting green. You just never know what might pop up."

THANK YOU . . .

TO ANDREW HARWELL, BARBARA LALICKI, and everyone at Harper who make writing these Riley Mack stories so much fun.

To J.J., my extremely talented (not to mention gorgeous) wife, who is the world's best first editor.

To my agent, Eric Myers.

To the city of Austin's Watershed Protection Department, Sara Heilman, and the middle school earth science teachers in Austin, Texas, who put together the Country Club Creek Ichthycide curriculum that taught me so much about investigating water pollution.

And to all the Known Troublemakers out there who stand up for what's right and defend those who cannot defend themselves.